RED RYDER
SECRET OF WOLF CANYON

RED RYDER

and the

SECRET OF
WOLF CANYON

Story by
S. S. STEVENS

Based on the Famous Newspaper Strip by
FRED HARMAN

WHITMAN PUBLISHING COMPANY
RACINE, WISCONSIN

CONTENTS

The Werewolf Leaped Savagely

RED RYDER

and the

SECRET OF WOLF CANYON

CHAPTER I

The sun dropped low in the west, below the jagged edge of Wolf Canyon, playing its fading light on the lazy, cumulus clouds drifting high over the rugged landscape. Suddenly, as though a black cape had been whipped across the sky, pitch-black night covered all, but the stillness that accompanied it was fraught with a tense expectancy.

A herd of cows watering at the southernmost end of Wolf Creek paused in their drinking; they tilted their heads, pointed up their ears and stood very still, as though waiting for something. When the sound came, clear and piercing through the night—the cry of a lone lobo wolf fast on a trail—the cows huddled close together and made frightened sounds deep in their throats.

The cry of the wolf echoed repeatedly through the canyon. It was a cry of death, and all living things within earshot trembled.

Who was next?

Every night for nearly a week the wolf had claimed a

victim.

Six nights had the wolf howled before the moon had risen; six torn, mangled bodies were mute testimony of his seeming invincibility.

Whose trail was the wolf tracking this night?

Jeb Weston and his wife, Mary, tucked their young son, Peter, into bed and retired to the kitchen of their small ranch house to chat and read the local Wolf Creek paper before turning in. Jeb scanned the paper with unseeing eyes, then slowly let it drop from his hand. He gazed blankly before him, deep in troubled thought.

"Jeb, what's the matter?" asked Mary.

"Dunno, Mary. Hadda funny feelin' all day, like I been watched."

He puffed deeply on his pipe, then glanced guiltily into his wife's worried eyes and forced a smile.

"Oh, 'tain't nothin'—guess these Wolf Creek murders are gettin' on my nerves," he said, pointing to the latest headline. "Forget it!"

"But, Jeb . . ."

Before she had a chance to say more, the ghostly cry of the lobo wolf rang through the night. Echoes of it seemed to hang forebodingly for a moment in the small close kitchen. The blood drained from Mary's face and she stared in alarm at her husband's strong impassive features. Only his sharp, sun-paled eyes showed the concern that struck through him like a thunderbolt.

The cry had come from close by, not more than half

a mile away.

"Ooooooooooooo," the wolf sound pierced the night again—closer!

A few seconds later, there was a knock on the door.

"Jeb!"

"Easy, Mary," said Jeb sharply, rising to his feet and taking his carbine from the wall rack. "Easy . . ."

The soft knock was repeated.

"Don't answer it, Jeb. I beg of you—don't answer it!"

Jeb cocked his carbine and moved to the door.

"Wolves don't knock on doors, Mary. Someone's askin' to come in," he said.

Jeb Weston slid the bolt and pulled open the door.

"Jeb, *please* be careful," cried Mary, starting to her feet.

"If some hombre's out there with that wolf on the trail, I'm not lettin' 'im stay out there to be mangled!"

Taking a firm grip on his carbine, he stepped into the open to greet his visitor. There was a soft swishing sound through the air, a quick thud. Cold steel had pierced Jeb Weston's heart. He fell against the door and slid to the ground, a surprised expression on his face.

Mary ran to the door in time to see Jeb fall. At the sight of a quivering knife protruding from his breast she froze with terror. For an instant, she watched her husband lying on the ground, forever stilled. He had gone to save someone from the fate that was now his. With a stifled cry she fell sobbing on his lifeless body.

"Jeb! . . . JEB!"

Only the taunting wolf cry answered her.

The following day, into the old cow town of Wolf Creek, situated on a mesa overlooking the broad rolling range country surrounding the scraggly canyon, rode an odd but familiar pair.

Mounted on a beautifully mottled black and white pinto—white-faced and with a black forelock—the first rider was a tall, broad-shouldered man, with slim flat hips, who rode the loping sway of his cayuse as a cork rides the easy swell of a quiet sea.

Crowning the man's long rawboned face with its slightly crooked nose and square chin, was a mop of the reddest hair in the whole Southwest country. His tanned, leathery, wind-cut complexion was in strange contrast to his flaming topper. Worry was reflected in his steel gray eyes as he moved up the center of the street. A pall seemed to have dropped over the townspeople. Red Ryder knew that tragedy had struck or was hovering over each one of them.

The second half of this strange team was a small bare-chested Indian boy with jet-black hair bobbed Indian-fashion, bound in inch-wide red ribbon with a single eagle feather stuck in the side. This was Little Beaver, Red Ryder's pal of the saddle. His feet, shod in soft moccasins, gently pressed his sure-footed Indian pony's taut sides, urging him to keep up with the longer lopes of his companion's full-sized pinto.

Reaching the one-story adobe building at the end of

the street—the sheriff's office and jail all in one—the two riders dismounted, hitched their horses to the post out front and sauntered toward the door.

The sound of angry voices reached their ears before they had taken two steps.

"I'm tellin' you, Sheriff, you gotta do somepin' pronto 'bout these Wolf Creek killin's," shouted a voice that Red Ryder recognized as that of Jeff Wilkins, Wolf Creek's banker and Number One citizen. "The wolf got poor Jeb Weston last night, an' Lord knows where it's gonna strike tonight!"

"Jeb Weston warn't killed by no wolf, Jeff," replied Sheriff Parks heatedly. "There was a knife struck plumb clean through his heart!"

"But those other killin's," insisted Jeff Wilkins. "What about them? Those bodies were clawed an' mangled almost beyond recognition. An' what's more, wolf tracks were found around each one!"

Red Ryder paused outside the door and motioned Little Beaver to do likewise. It was as good a time as any to get all the facts: to learn why he had been urgently summoned back to Wolf Creek.

"For that matter," Wilkins's voice continued, "wolf tracks were found outside Jeb Weston's house. You saw them yourself."

"I ain't one for believin' much in such tales, but mebbe," said the Sheriff, "mebbe it's a *werewolf!* I been told about that kind o' queer critter."

"A what?"

"Werewolf—I been told it's a man who, come night, changes his skin an' takes on the look an' habit of the wolf. Once he's changed, he lights out on a trail, huntin' to kill!"

"But that's just a yarn—y'know, superstition."

"I've heard tell o' stranger things 'n that, Jeff, an' people said they was superstition too—till they happened!"

The banker didn't answer immediately. He too had heard tales from people who claimed to be eye-witnesses; strange things that had happened on the range—things, the telling of which made the blood run cold. Memory of some of these stories gave him pause to think and wonder.

"Mebbe you're right, Sheriff," he said slowly in a cracked voice.

Red Ryder and Little Beaver heard the Sheriff first grunt and then sigh wearily. Little Beaver's knees, Red noted with a wry smile, were knocking against each other like a rattlesnake's rattlers when danger approaches.

Inside, Jeff Wilkins was yelling again. His voice had taken on a hysterical quality.

"If it is a werewolf, he might attack anybody—you, me! He's gotta be tracked down an' killed. What're ya sittin' here for? Why don'tcha git out an' hunt him down?"

The Sheriff plunked his feet down from the desk where they had been resting crossed over each other. He

Death Lurked Outside Their Home

swung around in his swivel chair and faced the whining banker with a contemptuous look.

"I'm waitin'," he said quietly with controlled anger, "I'm waitin' fer the one hombre capable of smokin' the critter out an' fillin' him fulla lead."

"Who's that?" asked the banker sarcastically.

"Calls himself Red Ryder," was the short answer.

"Red Ryder? Why, I thought he was . . ." Jeff Wilkins's voice broke off incredulously.

"Yes, Red Ryder. I sent him a telegram day 'fore yesterday, an' if I know Red, he's hightailin' it back here right now!"

"Truer words were never spoken, Sheriff!"

"Red!"

The Sheriff leaped from the chair and heaved his heavy muscular bulk across the room with surprising agility for such a massive man. He had spied his friend in need and grasped the rangy cowboy's hand in a bear-like grip and pumped it vigorously.

"Red, you ole hootin' coyote, you! You shore musta made that dust fly. I wasn't 'spectin' ya till 'bout noon tomorrow."

Red Ryder grinned warmly back at his old friend and returned the hearty handshake. "Well, when Little Beaver an' I got yore wire, we got mighty worried and rode a straight trail so's we'd get here as quick as possible."

"Howdy, Red," said Jeff Wilkins, standing by and smiling uncertainly. "We're sure glad to see your face round these parts again."

"Howdy," returned Red with a curt nod.

His steel grey eyes narrowed as he let them fall upon the banker's pudgy figure. There was no friendliness in either man's expression. Both had their reasons to eye each other with unmasked dislike. Wilkins shifted uneasily under Red's steady gaze and dropped his eyes.

Red's lip curled in disgust and he turned back to the Sheriff.

"What seems to be the trouble around here?" he asked. "Ghosts?"

"You ain't far off," answered the Sheriff unsmilingly. "One o' them there werewolves is loose in the canyon, Red, killin' right an' left. Last night he took his seventh victim—Jeb Weston."

If the word "werewolf" startled him, Red did not show it. He listened intently while the Sheriff told him of the mysterious murders terrorizing every inhabitant of the canyon. He gave no hint that he already knew most of the details.

Little Beaver stood close to Red, looking up at the Sheriff with big, coal-black eyes, his mouth hanging open. For a little shaver, Little Beaver was as brave as they came, but like all Indians, superstitious beliefs were drilled into him from birth, were almost his second nature.

"You no needum Red Ryder and Little Beaver," he stated when the Sheriff had finished his recital. "You needum Medicine Man. Chase evil spirit from canyon, make-um all well again."

"I wish it was as simple as that, Little Beaver," answered the Sheriff with a wan smile. "But this critter's flesh and blood, an' only hot lead from a quick .45 is gonna send him to Kingdom Come!"

" 'Fraid yo're right there, Sheriff," answered Red, touching his two Colt .45's hanging at his hips from low-slung holsters. "I guess Little Beaver and me will just ride out through the canyon a piece and see what we can smell out."

"Want me to come along?"

"No, thanks," replied Red, turning and making for the door with Little Beaver at his heels. "Might scare the varmint if too many of us set in. Come on, Little Beaver."

"Little Beaver come, but Little Beaver betchum hot tamale Red Ryder gonna wishum he talk first with Medicine Man!"

"When'll you be back, Red?" asked Sheriff Parks, following them outside.

" 'Long 'bout sundown," said Red, lifting himself into his high-backed saddle with an effortless motion. "See you then!"

He pulled Thunder's head about, touched his spurs to the horse's flank and galloped off. Little Beaver vaulted on his bareback pony and sped after him, tiny batwing chaps flapping in the wind.

Jeff Wilkins watched the two figures disappear in a cloud of dust. He linked his thumbs in his cartridge

belt and stood for a moment biting his short-cropped
mustache. A worried expression troubled his fat yellow-
ish face.

Red and Little Beaver sped over the mesa and reached
the dropping off place when the sun was overhead. They
reined in and gazed down at the scraggly landscape below, bright, glaring and clearly etched under the mid-
day sun.

It was strange country—a study in sharp contrasts. It
stretched for miles. As far as the eye could see were uneven, rocky sections, barren of vegetation of any sort,
jutting into the finest grazing land in the Southwest.

Small herds of cows dotted the grass sections, but over
on the north, as Red Ryder and Little Beaver well knew,
was a large range of hated sheep—the curse and ruin of
any cow country. Sheep eat the grass right down to its
roots, killing it. Wherever they go they leave an oily
stench from their hoofs which contaminates the land and
watering holes. After a sheep herd has passed over a
range, its use as grazing land for cattle is ended for years
to come.

It was no wonder, therefore, that the thought of those
sheep grazing the north section made Red Ryder's blood
boil. It brought to mind the bitter fight he and the small
ranchers of Wolf Creek had fought the previous year with
Sam Welt, who had bought the north section from banker Jeff Wilkins. This raw deal to the ranchers of Wolf
Creek was the reason Red had nothing but contempt

and hatred for the scheming banker.

Unfortunately, the law had been on Wilkins's and Welt's side. Wilkins had owned the property and it was his right to sell to whom he pleased. He refused to listen to the pleas of the ranchers and only laughed at their threats.

Finally, Red Ryder had taken up a collection of five thousand dollars from the small ranchers, who could hardly afford it with market prices dropping way down, and offered to buy the section from Welt. Without even giving the matter a moment's consideration, Welt had countered with a proposition to buy out all of the small ranches in the canyon country.

If his deal had been a fair one, Red and the ranchers might have considered it—but three dollars an acre for land that was easily worth twenty dollars, was ridiculous and insulting. They turned the proposition down flat and returned to their homes ready to fight.

Red realized that Welt and Wilkins wanted all Wolf Creek grazing land, and would stop at nothing to get it. For that reason he was not surprised to learn a few days later that Welt was building a dam across Wolf Creek to stop the water from flowing through the lower ranches. This meant death to the cattle and ruin to the ranches.

Range war was declared!

For four miserable, unhappy months, the cattlemen and sheepmen hunted and killed each other without mercy. Some of Red's closest friends among the cattlemen were murdered with bullets in their backs.

Though Red knew it was wrong—that fighting would get them nowhere—he had stuck with his friends. His roaring .45's and the clever fast action which he and Little Beaver put forth, were in a great part responsible for the cattlemen holding their own.

When no end seemed in sight; when death might be hidden behind any protecting rock; when the situation seemed absolutely hopeless—the miracle had happened. Word came through that the State Legislature had passed a law forbidding any person to dam up a water supply passing through land where cattle were grazing.

It had been one of the bitterest wars ever fought between sheepmen and cattlemen, mused Red, as he and Little Beaver looked down into the canyon. And the miracle that had saved the cattlemen he well knew was only temporary. Jeff Wilkins and Sam Welt weren't the kind to give up so easily. Laws were something that they used when they could be put to their advantage, and ignored when they stood in their way.

"Little Beaver have hunch cattle and sheep war not over yet!" said the little Indian boy, as though divining Red Ryder's thoughts. "Mebbe we hang round Wolf Creek we seeum some action. Yes, Red Ryder?"

Red Ryder smiled and shook his head.

"I shore hope not, Little Beaver. The ranchers in these parts has had enough fightin'. They're peaceable people, and if those sheepmen know what's good fer 'em, they'll

ride strict herd on their sheep and keep outa cattle country."

"Mebbe," said Little Beaver, shooting Red a sage look.
"But me thinkum Red Ryder know better."

He jerked his pony's reins and urged him into a quick
gallop. They covered the remaining distance to the edge
of the incline and bucked and slid their mounts down
the loose-graveled slope. The well-trained, sure-footed
animals hit their stride at the bottom and shot off into
the flat land.

Crrack!

The deadly sound of a rifle was accompanied by the
chilling whine of a bullet.

Red Ryder lurched from the saddle of his speeding
pinto and hit the ground hard. His body rolled and
bounced for a few yards and came to a motionless halt,
face downward!

CHAPTER II

SNIPER

At the whip-like crack of the rifle, Little Beaver instinctively ducked low, close to his pony's neck, and urged it to greater speed. The thudding bump of Red Ryder's body hitting the ground came to him over the dull beat of hooves in the soft, dusty terrain. He shot a quick glance over his shoulder, gasped and jerked hard on his reins. The pony reared to its hind legs and skidded in a cloud of dust for several feet before it could right itself and turn around.

Red Ryder lay in a heap, his pinto standing uncertainly over him, looking questioningly at Little Beaver as the Indian boy hopped from the pony's back and dropped to Red's side.

"Red Ryder . . . Red Ryder!" he screamed. "Talk to me . . . Tell Little Beaver yore not hurtum bad!"

"Take it easy, Little Beaver, I'm all right," answered the supposedly dead cowboy in a muffled voice. "I'm playin' 'possum to find out who tried to plug me."

"Whewwww! Me thoughtum you much dead. What you want Little Beaver should do?"

"Act like you think I'm done for. Then git on yore pony, take Thunder's reins and lead him away. Make fer those cottonwoods up ahead and wait in there for me," instructed Red, his head burrowed in his arms.

Little Beaver got slowly to his feet, looked long and sadly at the body of his "departed" benefactor, climbed dejectedly upon his pony's back, caught Thunder's reins and turned for one last look at Red Ryder. He rubbed his eyes with smudgy hands and turned his pony toward the cottonwoods.

His "play acting" had the desired effect. The second he disappeared into the clump of trees, a figure rose from a lying-down position on the edge of the mesa, looked down for a long moment at Red's lifeless body, disappeared from view, and returned an instant later riding a smoky, grey mustang. Easing the horse carefully down the slope, he paused every once in a while to study the prone figure sprawled in the hot sun on the dusty flats below. His movements were uncertain, as though he didn't quite trust his own eyesight. Obviously he feared that at any moment Red Ryder would be on his feet, blazing guns in hand, throwing hot lead at him.

When he reached the flat land, instead of riding directly toward Red, he circled around and approached from behind. His six-shooter rested menacingly on his saddle horn, aimed at a spot in the center of Red's uncovered head. He was taking no chances.

At fifty feet, he stopped, dismounted and gingerly stepped forward, six-shooter leveled at his hip. Still Red Ryder did not move.

From the cottonwood trees, Little Beaver watched the

drama with fearful eyes. As soon as he had seen the man rise on top of the mesa, he had unslung his bow from his back and fitted an arrow to it. With growing concern and worry, he watched the stranger descend to the flats, circle around, dismount and move cautiously toward Red Ryder, gun ready for action.

Little Beaver waited no longer. He pulled back on his bow string and took careful aim, following the man inch by inch.

When he stood over Red Ryder's motionless figure, the stranger let his gun fall to his side. A triumphant leer creased his cruel, lumpy, unshaved face. He set the toe of his boot underneath Red's chest and rolled him over.

Two wide-open eyes stared up at him—but not the expressionless eyes of a dead man! Before he had a chance to make a move, two guns blazed at him from the ground, knocking his shooter from his hand.

Red Ryder leaped to his feet, smoking guns still in hand, and was about to take his prisoner.

At the same instant, there was a singing twang. An arrow shot through the air and nearly found its mark.

Red was startled and half turned his head. He felt a push from behind. The stranger had grabbed his chance— he ran to his mustang, mounted, and rode off.

Red waved to Little Beaver to come out. The Indian boy hopped on his pony and raced out of the cottonwoods, leading Thunder.

"Little Beaver makeum fine shot, eh, Red Ryder?" he

asked proudly, as he reined up before his friend.

"You little varmint! Why'd ja hafta go and string an arrow at 'im?" retorted Red, angrily. "I wanted to talk to the hombre and find out who he's workin' fer!"

The small Indian boy slipped down from his pony and looked up petulantly at his hero.

"Little Beaver just wantum help his friend Red Ryder," he replied in a small voice.

"Little Beaver should know by this time Red Ryder don't need help 'less he asks fer it!"

"Me much sorry. Red Ryder forgive?"

Little Beaver looked up hopefully at the stern face towering above him. A happy smile lighted his features when he saw that—though the face was stern and unmoving—Red Ryder's eyes danced merrily.

"Good! . . . Good! . . . Red Ryder not angry any more!"

"Who says I ain't?"

"Yore eyes says so," laughed the little Indian. "Yore face like big black cloud which covers stars, but yore eyes twinkle through stern face like stars through clouds."

Red broke into a wide grin, bent down and whacked Little Beaver heartily on the lower end of his back.

"Git along, you tricky little heathen! Hop on that pony o' yours. We gotta make tracks and clear up this werewolf mystery." He caught Thunder's rein and swung into the saddle.

Little Beaver jumped to his pony's back, took a last

look at the scene, and puckered his lips in a tight smile.

"Me thinkum Red Ryder not spank very hard!" he muttered to himself, and followed Red Ryder across the plains at a fast gallop.

An hour's fast riding across the range brought them to the canyon proper. Three miles up-river was Jeb Weston's house which, Red naturally reasoned, was the logical place to start "smellin' 'round"—as he put it.

Following a shelf-path on the canyon's rim, they picked their way up a rocky crevice and found themselves after a while looking out on a broad spread of about five hundred acres.

In the center of the spread was a small ranch house, paint-peeled, warped and sagging from long exposure to the hot sun and other elements. About a hundred feet back of it was a small gathering of people. They kneeled with bared heads, bowed in grief, around a pine-board coffin standing on the edge of a freshly dug grave. A tall, gaunt figure stood in their midst, holding a Bible in his hands and reading from the text.

Mary Weston kneeled sobbing beside the coffin, her young son, Peter, pressed beside her, frightened and tearful.

Quietly, Red Ryder and Little Beaver approached. Not wishing to disturb the funeral ceremony, they dismounted in the shadows of the house and waited. Red saw among the mourners many of his friends, come to pay their last respects to their fellow rancher, Jeb Weston, and to comfort and help Mary Weston in her hour of trial.

Many of their women folk were also there, dressed in black—an all too familiar raiment in Wolf Canyon during the past year. It seemed, Red mused, that a cloud of doom had dropped over the once prospering and happy section with the importation of the sheep. Now it had struck a second time—but in a way a thousand times more awful than the sheep war of the previous year. It struck mysteriously, with the cunning of a beast and the intelligent planning of a human being; a combination which gave the bravest and most capable man little chance to defend himself.

Sheriff Parks was not the only one who voiced the werewolf theory. Others were beginning to have the same fearful suspicion. Even as Red Ryder and Little Beaver stood watching, Red noticed the men and women looking furtively under shaded eyelids at their neighbors. He could almost read the question in each one's mind:

"Is this man next to me the Werewolf—the terrible monster who killed Jeb Weston?"

Red Ryder realized in a flash the seriousness of the situation. These small ranchers were dependent upon each other in a hundred ways. Trusting and helping their neighbors, and being helped in turn, was the only chance they had individually of succeeding in the unequal task of making their ranches pay. Once this trust was lost— the helping-hand spirit replaced by fear and suspicion—

all was lost and the cattlemen would find themselves bankrupt, and finally driven out of their very homes.

Fear is a terrible instrument. Raised to a fever pitch, it manifests suspicion, selfishness and hatred. The were-wolf fear already had gripped the Canyon; suspicion was evidencing itself; soon this very group of mourners might well be hating and hunting each other like wild beasts.

Still unnoticed as he watched, and pursued his thoughts, Red Ryder resolved to end this werewolf myth; to track down and kill the beast, whatever it was, even if his life was the forfeit. These people—his friends—were totter-ing on the brink of self destruction. That he proposed to sacrifice himself for a cause in which he had no stakes of his own, didn't enter Red's mind; his life was dedi-cated to helping others when danger and destruction threatened.

When the coffin was lowered and the earth covered over, Red and Little Beaver walked from the shadows straight toward Mary Weston. At the sight of the tall lean cowboy, Mary struggled to her feet, stumbled a few steps, and fell sobbing into his arms.

Clumsily, but gently, Red patted her head and firmly gripped her arm. The silent pressure of his strong fin-gers expressed more than words his deep feeling over her loss. When her sobs quieted, he held her from him and gazed into her eyes with a look that said, "Courage, Mary —courage!"

"Red, you heard about Jeb?"

"Yes, Mary. That's why Little Beaver an' me is here."

"But yo're too late! Jeb's dead—killed by that—that horrible *werewolf!*" she cried.

"I'm—I'm sorry, Mary."

"Oh, Red—'tain't yore fault. I don't know what I'm sayin'. But what about these people?" she said suddenly, pointing to the silent group who stood about with fear stamped on their brows. "An' what about me and Peter? The Werewolf is gonna strike again tonight! It might be one of us!"

"I don't hold with this werewolf business, Mary," answered Red quietly, eyeing the whole group. "I been thinkin' 'bout it all the way out an' ever since I got here. 'Pears to me you people're lettin' yore 'maginations sort o' run away with you. The critter that's been spillin' blood ain't no more'n a foul-smellin', bloodthirsty lobo wolf, or—"

Red paused and looked uncertainly at the faces about him.

"Or what?" demanded Sam Locke, a neighboring rancher.

"Or," Red continued in a sharp tone, "some crawlin' varmint who's tryin' to scare the daylights out o' the lotta you and force you out o' the Canyon!"

There was a surprised silence for a moment. The ranchers exchanged quick, puzzled looks.

"There ain't no sane man could be so low as to claw an' mangle a man to death, Red," retorted Sam. "The

wolf tracks 'round each victim speak for themselves.
Maybe like you say, it's a lobo wolf, but me an' the boys
doubt it."

"Yo're fergettin' about Jeb, ain'tcha? He warn't clawed
to death," Red argued. "I never heard tell o' a knife-
throwin' wolf!"

"But a werewolf might throw a knife, Red," put in
Mary.

Red hitched his holsters, and shook his head stubborn-
ly. Still, it was no use wasting time arguing. It was getting late and he wanted to scout the ranch with Little
Beaver and try to pick up the wolf's trail. The only way
to convince these frightened people was to come to grips
with the Killer.

"I don't aim to settle this thing with talk," said Red.
"Little Beaver an' me is gonna smell it out. When we do,
I'm bettin' yo're gonna be a mighty surprised bunch o'
folk learnin' what's really behind these killin's."

"Mebbe yo're right, Red. Hope you are. An' if you're
wantin' a posse to ride with you, the boys here an' me is
ready," answered Sam, speaking for the group, who nodded silently.

Red ran his eyes over the gruff, honest faces about him
and smiled. Despite their fears, they were brave men,
ready to tackle even what they believed to be something
supernatural. Furthermore, riding posse that night would
mean leaving their women folk and children alone and
unprotected against the horrible danger.

"No," he said, after a while, "you all go home, bar yore doors and don't answer for no one till sun-up. Me an' Little Beaver can work better alone anyway."

Little Beaver gulped and nodded his head shakily. He was ready, as always, to follow Red Ryder anywhere, but this time his heart wasn't in it. In order to cover up his trembling, he threw out his bare, muscular little chest and strutted before the group bravely.

"S-Sure! Me an' Red Ryder h-hunt W-Werewolf 'lone," he stuttered. "Bringum its pelt back to you by sun-up sure!"

The kindly folk chuckled at this brave assertion and moved to the corral to get their horses and wagons. Suddenly, Red's eyes narrowed and he turned to Mary, who was standing beside him watching the ranchers depart. "Ain't Russ Bellows been 'round to pay his respects, Mary?"

"Russ? . . . Why, let me think," replied Mary, wrinkling her brow. "No, he ain't been here, come to recollect. Why?"

"Peculiar, Russ an' Jeb bein' such good friends," said Red in a tight voice. "Yo're sure he's all right? Ain't been attacked or nothin'?"

"He was all right yesterday."

"How do you know?"

"He an' Jeb rode out all day collectin' strays."

Red's long, sharp, plain face lined with worry.

"I think I better ride over to his ranch first thing," he

muttered, "and make shore he's all right. Livin' alone like he does, he could be dead fer a week, and nobody'd know the difference."

When Red Ryder and Little Beaver were on their mounts, ready to go, Mary reached up and took Red's hand.

"You an' Little Beaver be careful, Red. Don't let what happened to—to Jeb, happen to you."

"Don't you worry yore pretty head, Mary," said Red with a slight smile. "Me and the little fellow can take care o' ourselves. The important thing is that you keep those doors and windows barred and don't let no one make you open 'em up! Savvy?"

"Savvy, Red. Good luck!" she called.

The sun was dipping low as they rode off. Mary watched them disappear over a knoll, riding into the fiery half ball of the sun shooting streaks of orange as it settled below Wolf Mountain.

Realizing for the first time that darkness was almost upon them, Mary took her small son, Peter, and hurried into the house. She barred all doors and windows as Red Ryder had instructed, and set about preparing the evening meal. Not realizing what she was doing, she set the usual three places at the kitchen table.

"Ooooooooooooooo."

At the hungry, bloodthirsty cry, a shudder convulsed her body, and she clasped Peter to her. It was then her eyes fell on the table set for three, and focused on the place which never again would be filled.

Her aching sobs drowned the wolf cry, which again this night was not far away.

CHAPTER III

ATTACK

"There it is!" shouted Red Ryder over his shoulder to Little Beaver, whose pony pounded at the heels of Red's longer-strided pinto.

The tall rider referred to the deadly sounding wolf cry echoing through the black night. It was the first time either of them had heard it, and even to their shock-calloused nerves it had a paralyzing effect.

There was an almost human quality to the weird tones, undulating in a mocking salute to the next victim. Unconsciously, Red and Little Beaver spurred their mounts to greater speed. They pounded through the grazing lands, skirted a herd of tense cattle who softly noised their fear, struggled up a winding path to a slanting mesa upon which Ress Bellows' house and range were located.

The wolf cry followed them, drawing nearer. Red slipped his carbine from its saddle holster and pulled in his horse. Little Beaver shot ahead. If the wolf did attack, he didn't want Little Beaver to be the first victim. Red could hear him muttering Indian talk into his mount's ear. Even at this moment of peril, Red could not help smiling.

They were passing over a rocky formation now. Suddenly Red's sharp ears detected a new note aside from

The Tracks Were Mysterious

the rapid clop-clop of their horses' hooves on the hard surface. A half mile farther on was Russ's house. He could see a light in the window and knew that Russ must be there.

A plan of action shot through Red's mind. He shouted to Little Beaver to make for Russ's house and not to stop for anything. Then his eye fastened on a broad rock about five feet high just ahead. He jumped to a crouched position on his saddle, holding tight on the reins ready to spring.

Red's pinto, Thunder, well trained, responded to his master's slightest touch and continued to pound over the rocky surface without a break in his stride. A few feet from the fast-nearing rock, Red uncoiled his sinewy muscles in a mighty leap. He hit the rock on his feet, but the force of his spring sent him spinning across its surface off balance. Vainly, he tried to right himself—crashed down.

Sharp pain and dancing lights spread through Red's head. After the first jarring shock, blackness seemed to force itself down on him from all directions. He felt his muscles grow relaxed and unresponsive.

Gritting his teeth, he fought against the numbness that was possessing his entire body. Through it he was aware of one thing—the new sound he had heard was near; the sound of sharp claws scratching against hard rock as they sped over the surface! It was very close now and slackening speed.

The beast's sharp nostrils had smelt the human being that was close by! Red's benumbed senses knew this and knew that unless he could pull himself quickly out of his dazed condition, he would be the eighth victim to be sacrificed in as many days.

Still his muscles refused to move. He heard the beast scratching below. Then he heard the cry—loud, piercing, as though right beside him. The horrible quality of the sound shocked Red's nerves into awareness. His muscles jerked spasmodically and came to life. At the same time, his head cleared.

His return to full consciousness was not a second too soon!

A long, dark shape vaulted through the air and landed at Red's feet before he had a chance to make a move. Red's hands darted with lightning speed to the mahogany handles of the guns at his hip, as he raised himself for the attack. They cleared leather and were cocked in a single motion.

The next instant, the beast was upon him, foul-smelling breath hot in his face. Red had no time to fire a shot. The dripping white fangs snapped. Red threw his right arm up in time to protect his throat and slammed the snout hard with the heavy gun.

The wolf roared with pain and slashed at Red's arm with his sharp, talon-like claws. Red felt the arm sear red hot with pain. He struggled to get his other gun arm around into the beast's side, so he could send a bullet through the hide into its heart. Keeping his throat protected with the wounded arm, and pounding the snout time and again, he finally worked his left arm around so that the muzzle of the gun rested in the spot over the heart.

He was so weak by this time that he could not pull the trigger. His mind told him he must—*he must!* Some unknown power like a second wind seemed to come to his aid, and the trigger finger slowly squeezed.

The loud blast from his gun hardly made an impression upon him. He sank into another world, everything going completely black this time. He made no effort to fight it off and accepted it with relief.

The moon rose over the mesa and all was very still. The wolf lay on top of Red Ryder, almost completely covering him. The blood from the hole in its side had poured out and spread along the rock in dark, twisting rivulets.

Red's first sensation when he came to, was one of heaviness over his entire body. Then the searing pain in his right arm brought him sharply to his senses and he opened his eyes. Staring him full in the face with lifeless eyes was the ghastly face of the wolf. Dried foam speckled his snout and flabby lips. The two extended fangs shone white, smooth and sharp.

Red shuddered and tried to roll over. In his weakened condition, the weight of the enormous beast was too much. He lay quietly for an instant, summoning a burst

of strength. The pain in his arm was torture. Fitting
his left arm under the wolf's body, he tensed his muscles
and lifted, rolling from under the beast at the same time.

Free of the burden, he lay panting for a time, and then
got slowly to his feet. It took him a little time to steady
himself; to shake off the rocking feeling in his head.
The wolf lay at his feet, fully six feet long from the snout
to the claws of the hind legs—the biggest lobo wolf
Red had ever seen. A sharp whistle sang threw his teeth.
No wonder Wolf Creek settlers had thought the beast
a werewolf.

After a close examination to see if there was anything
about the beast which would identify it as anything but
an overgrown lobo with a taste for human blood, he rose,
certain there was not. Gathering up his guns, he searched
for his carbine and found it stuck in a crevice where it
must have landed when it flew from his hand.

Every muscle of his body ached, and the wound in his
arm was more painful than ever. He set his eyes toward
the house about half a mile away, and noticed with
satisfaction that a light still burned in the window. Little
Beaver was there with Russ Bellows, safe and sound.
That at least was a source of satisfaction.

He scrambled down from the rock, keeping his right
arm pocketed inside his shirt front, Napoleon fashion.
With dragging steps, he made his way toward the house,
wishing that Thunder would come out and meet him
so he could ride the rest of the way.

Playing a hunch, he fitted his fingers to his lips and blew two shrill blasts. Much to his surprise, the soft thud of hoof beats answered the summons, and in a minute he was on Thunder's back, patting the loyal pinto. The horse had sensed his master's danger, and come back to wait until he was needed.

A few minutes later, he was in front of the house.. Little Beaver threw open the door and rushed out to meet him.

"Red Ryder? . . . That you, Red Ryder?" he shouted.

"It's me, young 'un. What's all the fuss?"

"Come quick. Russ very sick man. Die soon. Him want make talk with you first."

Despite his pain, Red slid quickly from the saddle and hurried into the house. It was dimly lit by a kerosene lantern hanging near the window, over a rough-hewn bed made of planks and padded with straw.

Russ Bellows lay on the bed very still. Even as Red Ryder came through the door, he could see the mutilated condition of the man's face; torn and stripped with ugly gashes such as the claws of a giant beast would make. The clothes on his body were ripped to shreds and stuck to him with clotted blood from the many wounds on his body.

"When did this happen?" Red asked Little Beaver.

"Last night, Russ say."

The dying man's eyes flickered open as Red stood over him. He raised a weak hand and motioned Red to kneel beside him. Painfully, Red dropped to his knees and leaned close to hear what Russ Bellows had to say.

The man worked his tongue over dry, cracked lips and tried to speak. For a moment, only hacking spurts of tortured breath sounded from his throat. Red leaned closer, aware that the man was trying to tell him something urgent with the last breaths he had in his body.

"Easy, Russ. Take yore time . . ."

"Got no time," he whispered. "Number's—up. Listen close . . ."

"I'm listening . . ."

"Werewolf—loose. I know who it—is."

"There ain't no werewolf, Russ. It's a real lobo an' I just killed it."

"No . . . No!" insisted the dying man. "There is—werewolf. Did this—to me last—night. I rec—o'nized him!"

"Yo're sure?"

"Certain! . . . He called me—by name—'fore he—attacked!"

Russ Bellows' breath came in short struggled pants at the recollection. He tried to raise himself up, but sank back at the gentle pressure of Red Ryder's hand.

Red looked up at Little Beaver questioningly.

"Who'd he say it was?" he asked the Indian boy.

"No say. Wanted to wait till Red Ryder came," replied Little Beaver with a slight shrug.

"Who is it, Russ?" said Red Ryder turning back to

the dying man.

"It's—it's . . ."

A gurgling sound escaped from the man's throat. For one awful second he stared up at Red, straining to whisper the name. Then the eyes glazed over, the body sank deeper into the straw and Red felt the man's hand drop palm outward.

Russ Bellows was dead!

Little Beaver mumbled a short verse in Indian language and raised both arms to the sky; a prayer and gesture to the Almighty Manitu to take the spirit of Russ Bellows into the Happy Hunting Ground. Red waited respectfully until the prayer was over, and then rose painfully to his feet and covered Russ's entire body with an old blanket.

"Russ good man," said Little Beaver, when this was done.

"Yes, Little Beaver, a good man who never did anyone any harm."

They stood silently for a moment, remembering the jovial, good-natured Russ Bellows, who always had time to do someone a favor.

Little Beaver gave a start when he noticed for the first time Red's mangled arm.

"Yore arm very sick. Little Beaver fix!"

With trained efficiency, Little Beaver washed the wounds and applied some herb salves to them, which he took from a little packet at his waist. Red winced during

the painful operation, but didn't utter a sound. When
the arm was bandaged, the searing pain was gone and
only a dull ache reminded him that he had come mighty
close to losing the limb altogether.

Though sore and weary from the trying events of the
day and the long journey behind, Red and Little Beaver
took Russ Bellows' body out underneath the stars, dug a
shallow grave and buried him. Red said a brief prayer
and put a crossed stick at the grave's head.

When the simple funeral ceremony was over, the man
and Indian boy talked of plans for the next day. The mystery grew more and more complicated.

"Little Beaver, I'll bet you all th' gold in these hills that
there's more'n one werewolf, or whatever varmints they
are, doin' all these killin's," Red asserted.

"Mebbe so, Red Ryder. But one werewolf can killum
you just as dead as other one. Werewolf almost get you
tonight."

"Listen, young 'un, that carcass out there's just an ord'-
nary lobo's body! Once I read somethin' about werewolves. The old stories said six-shooters and knives won't
kill 'em. Well, I shore plugged that varmint tonight with
my six-shooter, and it finished him just like any other
wolf," answered Red.

Without bothering to take off his boots, he bedded
down on the floor of the cabin and fell asleep immediately. Little Beaver stretched at his feet and quickly followed
his example.

No sooner were they quietly snoring than a head rose up and peered through the window. It was a cruel, grinning wolf head, foam dripping from its fangs. The two eyes blazed green through the darkness and stared for a long time at the two sleeping figures.

CHAPTER IV

At the crack of dawn, Red Ryder and Little Beaver turned out feeling greatly refreshed. Red's damaged arm, however, pained feverishly. After a quick breakfast of strong black coffee and dry biscuits, Little Beaver bathed, doctored and redressed the wound.

"Yo're a mighty good doctor, Little Beaver," said Red, admiringly, flexing the damaged arm when the dressing was in place.

"Not me good doctor. Herb medicine good doctor," answered the Indian boy modestly, blushing all the same. "Medicine Man of my tribe teachum me how to makeum when me small boy."

Red suppressed a smile at this inference that he was now a *big* boy. Hardly standing over four feet ten inches tall, Little Beaver had, for his tender years, led a life filled with such adventure as the average man did not experience in an entire life span. His brown little body was as hard as nails, well knit and well proportioned.

To Red Ryder, Little Beaver was more than an adopted son; he was his pal, companion and confidant. Together, they braved adventure and death—either would gladly sacrifice his life for the other.

Now, this morning, as the sun burst resplendently over

the slanting mesa of rich grazing land, the tie that bound
this white man and Indian boy together was stronger
than ever in the face of the inexplicable mystery they
were trying to solve. Last night, when they thought they
had cleared up the mystery of Wolf Creek Canyon, they
had learned from the dying lips of Russ Bellows that
their hunt was only beginning.

It was hard to believe Russ's statement that the creature had called him by name before launching its horrible attack. It was terrible to think that the creature was
someone he had known—someone the canyon folk probably knew and accepted as a normal human being. To all
outward appearances, the man was (if the werewolf
legend were true) normal until sundown. Then a horrible transformation came over him—long claws sprout-
ed from his hands and feet; a covering of coarse black
hair matted his body; his head became elongated and
pointed like the head of a wolf; and his eyes changed
from a human coloring to a blazing green. When the
metamorphosis was complete, he dropped to the ground
on all fours and became in every respect a hunting, clawing, bloodthirsty beast.

It was a vile, nauseating picture. The possibility that
it might be true caused Red to shudder. But his intelligence insisted that he search for a logical, human reason
for the killings.

Not so, Little Beaver. His superstitious mind, nurtured
on folk tales of his own people, could well believe in the

existence of a werewolf. He expressed his beliefs to Red Ryder and hoped that his friend could prove he was wrong and stem the flood of fear that coursed through his veins.

"I ain't sayin' one way or the other, Little Beaver," replied Red Ryder in a worried voice. "There's a sayin' that truth's stranger than fiction. Mebbe this is one o' those times."

Not even Red Ryder's intelligence could dispel the unmistakable signs which met their eyes the moment they stepped out of doors. All around the house were wolf tracks, not many hours old. Scratchings on the wood around the window showed that the wolf had stood on his hind legs looking inside the house. Indian boy and white man shuddered to think how close they had come to death, unaware of their danger.

They thought of their horses and ran to the rear of the house, across the short stretch to the barn. The wolf tracks led right up to it. They pulled open the heavy doors with trembling hands, and looked inside. The tracks followed right through.

"Look!" gasped Little Beaver.

"Trim my bunions with a dull ax!" exclaimed Red.

Blinking their eyes, they stood in the door for fully two minutes without saying another word, just staring at their cayuses. The animals pulled their noses from their feed boxes and looked back at them, swishing their tails in greeting. Each animal shone fresh and glossy, burrs, dust and grime expertly brushed from their hides. The floor of their stalls was bedded down with clean hay and, on a peg, Red Ryder's ornately tooled saddle shone bright, the leather rubbed with saddle grease, the silver Indian ornaments polished to a high gloss.

"Little Beaver," muttered Red. "Did you walk in yore sleep last night?"

"Red Ryder know Little Beaver don't like to workum so much he walk in sleep to do it!" replied the dumb-founded Indian boy.

"Who coulda done all this fer us then?" breathed Red.

Little Beaver pointed to the multiple tracks on the sod floor leading in and out of the stalls and around the barn.

"W-Werewolf!" he stammered.

Red Ryder simply nodded and felt, for the first time in his life, a spooky feeling akin to fear. It was not the fear of a man ready to run from danger; it was merely an uncertain feeling in the face of a grave task which had to be performed, but for which he had not the knowledge.

Red Ryder gloried in the challenge of any man or beast, for he knew how to fight, how to think, how to act quickly. But would all, or any of this, avail in a contest with a being possessed of supernatural powers?

There was only one way to find out.

"Little Beaver, that thing an' me is gonna meet up one o' these days soon," muttered Red in a voice edged with steel. "When we do, only one o' us is gonna walk away alive!"

Little Beaver felt sick inside at the thought of this meeting. There was little doubt in his mind who would come out the victor. If only he could persuade Red Ryder to give up this hunt—get as far away from Wolf Creek as possible!

But even as the thought was born in his mind, the Indian lad dismissed it, knowing full well that he could never turn Red Ryder from a sworn duty. And though Little Beaver did not realize it, his own bravery equaled his friend's. The werewolf struck genuine terror in him, but despite this, he had no thought of leaving Red's side, come death and destruction from a thousand directions.

When each had finished with his separate thoughts, one pressing question remained in their minds: *Why had the werewolf, whose instinct was to kill, tended the horses with such sympathetic care?*

"Why you thinkum, Red Ryder?"

"We gotta remember the werewolf's a man. Livin' in this country, he's been 'round horses all his life, like all o' us," answered Red, slowly pondering the question. " 'Pears to me like his love fer hoss flesh is the only decent instinct left in him when he changes to werewolf . . . Leastwise, that's the way I figure it."

The animals stamped impatiently in their stalls, anxious to have their masters come to them and stroke their sleek sides. Their tails swished and they neighed invitingly. This play for attention snapped Red and Little Beaver out of their dark thoughts. They grinned and hurried over to their frisky mounts.

Soon they were on their way, galloping back over the trail they had traveled in the dark.

"We'll find the body o' that wolf I killed on that rock up ahead," shouted Red Ryder. "We'll skin it and bring the pelt in like you promised."

"Wish it was werewolf's pelt," Little Beaver shouted back. "Mebbe we bring him in tomorrow, eh, Red Ryder?"

Red grinned and pulled in on his reins. Sawing gently on the left bit, he sidled Thunder up to the rock where, only a few hours before, Red had been in a death struggle with the vicious wolf. Little Beaver kneed up on his pony's back to get a better look over the ledge.

For the second time that morning, they stared at what they saw in open-mouthed astonishment. The carcass of the wolf was still there, *but skinned and headless!* Bloody wolf tracks covered the entire rock.

They were not the tracks of the dead beast, since the tracks were in its blood. Furthermore, Red had made certain the animal was stone dead before he left. Dead wolves didn't rise and walk around!

Red Ryder studied the skinned carcass intently. His eyes narrowed and the deep lines in his gaunt face grew rigid. What possible use did a werewolf have for a wolf pelt?—he asked himself.

"Come on, Little Beaver!" cried Red, wheeling his

horse around. "We got some mighty urgent trailin' to do!"

"We gonna follow up-um werewolf tracks—*now?*" gulped the tiny Indian.

"Now!"

Little Beaver kicked his heels into the pony's flanks and skeetered after Red Ryder. The man and boy kept their eyes peeled to the ground as they followed the bloody tracks over the rock surface, and into the alkaline ground beyond where the trail grew faint and hard to follow. A wind had evidently sprung up during the night, covering it over with dust.

They reached the slope down off the mesa and began a slow descent. There was a mixture of tracks in the soft sliding ground: horses' and wolves'. Little Beaver dropped from his pony, studied the ground carefully. A puzzled look crossed his face. He got down on his hands and knees, crawled around like a prairie dog looking for his hole.

"What's eatin' you, Little Beaver?" said Red, leaning over his saddle horn cross-armed, and squinting at a spot Little Beaver seemed to be concentrating upon.

"Tracks much strange. Can't understand."

"How so?"

"Two wolves climb hill last night," said Little Beaver, pointing to two sets of separate imprints. "But only *one* wolf come down." He pointed to a third set of prints.

Red nodded. "So?"

"Front leg tracks for wolf who come down not here. Only hind leg tracks like two leg animal!" replied Little Beaver. "Werewolf, come down hill like you an' me. *He stand up!*"

Red's brow furrowed, but only for a moment. As Little Beaver said, there were only hind leg prints running down. Furthermore, the prints were deep and broad, unlike those of a four-legged beast.

A cold smile creased Red's lips. He looked up from the ground and off into the distance, toward the rocky crests. Somewhere, within the range of his view, whatever made those tracks was hiding out for the day. It could not have traveled far, he was certain. Man or beast, in the space of but a few hours, can cover little ground *traveling upright on only two feet!*

His sun-paled eyes contemplated the rocky formations on the horizon. The contours, the trails, the caves and secrets of each one were well known to him and Little Beaver. All of them were wild, harsh and yielding nothing—dead parts of a living world.

Red studied them all, dismissed each one in turn as being a likely hiding place for the werewolf. Finally, he turned his eyes north. A large blob of rock pierced the sky and fell away in a series of sharp needle-like summits. It was the most uninviting formation of them all, but Red remembered that, nestled at its base on the far side, was a valley of rich soil, watered by a subterranean river which came to the surface at this point.

Clay Lerner had owned that piece of grazing land and used it for homesteading. He had been a good fellow, Red recalled, throwing his lot in with the cattlemen during the sheep war the previous year. He had been reported killed and his wife had stayed on at the farm, taking up his work where he had left off.

"Someone come!" said Little Beaver, pointing to a cloud of dust heading toward them from the south.

Red swept his eyes around.

"Looks like a posse," he said.

"Come from Wolf Creek way," answered Little Beaver, squinting at the horsemen. "Come to fetchum you an' me."

Red darted a puzzled look at his small companion.

"Fetch us? What in tarnation makes you think that?" he demanded.

"Red tellum Sheriff Parks he be back to Wolf Creek come sun-down last night. Red kinda late an' Sheriff get worried. He think Red Ryder an' Little Beaver at bottom o' werewolf's stomach!"

Red grinned and chuckled softly.

"Clean forgot all about it," he said. "I wonder if Jeff Wilkins is ridin' with 'em. He's one hombre who's hopin' an' wishin' that all they're gonna find left o' us is a few cracked bones."

"He mighty mean man," said Little Beaver, vaulting to his pony's back.

"Mighty mean," answered Red; then added slyly, "He's

what you'd call a werewolf in sheep's clothes."

Little Beaver fixed Red with a sour look and said: "Red Ryder make-um bum joke so early in morning."

They rode toward the fast approaching posse at a leisurely pace. Red's expression was happy and carefree for the first time since they had arrived back in Wolf Creek. He even hummed a cowboy chanty in his stringent baritone, causing Little Beaver to wrinkle his nose in disgust.

"Red Ryder also sing bum in morning," he said, supplementing his other remark.

Red grinned and waved at the posse, now within hailing distance.

"That you, Red?" shouted Sheriff Parks from the distance.

" 'Tain't the ghost you expected to be pickin' up," called Red, cupping his hand to his mouth.

"You an' Little Beaver okay?"

"Shore are!"

"Good!"

The horsemen met and there was some good-natured joshing. But behind the gaiety, Red detected an anxious note in all their voices. Though they laughed, their eyes questioned. In some of them, Red saw fear.

"What in blazes happened to you, Red?" asked Sheriff Parks. "You said you'd be back by sun-down last night."

Red rolled in his saddle and smiled.

"Wal, it's this way, Sheriff," he said. "Me an' yore werewolf had a little date to sorta get acquainted."

"You mean, you met up with it?"

The ranchers pushed forward in their saddles, crowding close to Little Beaver and Red. Hope shown from their faces. If Red had survived a meeting with the beast, then it was not beyond the realm of possibility that he could slay it.

"Well, what happened?" someone shouted.

"We didn't exactly meet the critter," replied Red, "but he was sniffin' at our door when we was sleepin' over to Russ Bellows's."

"Say, how is Russ?" put in Sheriff Parks. "Mary Weston told me you was ridin' over to see him."

"Russ is dead!"

A startled mumble ran through the crowd. Red's sharp eyes darted from one face to the other, searching for some sign. It wasn't improbable that someone there knew of Russ Bellows's death, but no face betrayed such a sign. Either every man there was innocent, or one of them was a good actor.

The face Red searched most intently, the face he despised—the face of the only man whom he deeply suspected, showed no more, and no less than the others. Jeff Wilkins met Red's eyes unwaveringly.

"Yes," continued Red, "Russ was mangled and torn almost beyond recognition."

"When?" asked the Sheriff.

"Night 'fore last."

A shadow fell over Sheriff Parks's face and he moved his horse closer to Red's, leaning over in his saddle to whisper into Red's ear.

"Red, that means two people was killed that night— Jeb Weston and Russ Bellows. But they was killed different ways!"

"That's what I been thinkin', Sheriff," said Red.

They moved their horses apart from the others and carried on a conversation in low, guarded tones.

"You thinkin' what I'm thinkin', Red?" muttered the Sheriff.

"If it's that, we got more on our hands than a werewolf—yes!"

Sheriff Parks nodded, his face screwed up in deep thought. "That knife killin' o' Jeb Weston ain't ever set natural-like in my mind. Can't see why the critter should change his tactics."

"I don't think he did, Sheriff," answered Red, pushing his flat-crowned, broad-brimmed Stetson off his face. "Jeb Weston's killin' means we're up against something entirely different."

Out of the corner of his eye, Red noticed Jeff Wilkins backing towards them, out of the circle of men talking to Little Beaver. He was leaning back in his saddle, his head slightly turned, his ear cocked to pick up traces of whispered conversation. Red warned the Sheriff with a look and they moved back into the circle.

Red eyed Wilkins narrowly as he passed him. The

man's face was a mask. Red wondered if he had heard anything. Whether he had or had not, Red decided that from then on it would be a good idea to keep an eye on the banker.

"Little Beaver tells us you killed a wolf last night, Red," said Len Parks, the Sheriff's son, eagerly. "Did he show any traces of werewolf?"

"Sorry to disappoint you, but it was just a stray lobo who got our scent and went after us," Red replied with a smile. "Now, I think you all better be gettin' back to yore ranches and let Little Beaver and me get back to work."

They turned their horses to go, but Jeff Wilkins lagged behind. "If you'll be needin' some o' my fightin' boys, Red, just say the word."

"What makes you think I'll be needin' 'em, Wilkins?" retorted Red, fixing the fat banker with an unconcealed look of suspicion and distrust.

Wilkins's face became dark for a moment at the contempt in Red's voice, but he covered it up with a big smile which showed his fang-like, tobacco-stained teeth.

"Now wait a minute, Red!" he begged. "This ain't no time for you an' me to be arguin' differences over cattle land an' sheep land. This werewolf is a menace to everybody. Me an' my boys want to help clean him out just as much as you an' the cattlemen."

Red's expression didn't change.

"Look, Red, my boys are blood an' flesh just like the

rest o' you. That werewolf ain't particular whether it's sheepmen or cattlemen he's settin' his teeth into. See it our way," he urged. "We gotta right to help just as much as anybody."

"I wonder," answered Red, turning Thunder away. "It looks mighty peculiar that only cattlemen has met up with him so far!"

He touched his spurs into Thunder's belly and was off, with Little Beaver flying in his wake. Wilkins sat watching him, cursing under his breath. His hand wandered toward the heavy shooter at his hip. Red was a perfect target. But Jeff Wilkins didn't do his own killing. He hired men for that.

Red and Little Beaver headed due north. The sun was high now and beating down on them relentlessly. The hot wind was filled with dust, and soon their faces were streaked and dirty. Occasionally, they passed a herd of grazing cattle, a few strays. Around noon they approached Zeth Todd's ranch house.

Zeth, coming in from the range for lunch, met and invited them to rest up their horses and have a bite. Mrs. Todd was delighted to see Red, as also was her son, Danny. Red was Danny's godfather and also his hero. Someday he hoped to ride the West with Red and Little Beaver and share their adventurous life.

"Where you headin', Red?" asked Zeth, when lunch was over.

"Needle Rock."

"It's a funny thing," Zeth said after a moment. "Ever since Clay Lerner died, his wife ain't rid over to see my missus."

"Must take up all her time farmin' that land," put in Mrs. Todd, a roly-poly, good-natured little woman. "Land sakes, I don't see how she does it all by herself."

"By herself?" retorted Zeth, looking at his wife in surprise. "She's got a hand helpin' her. I see him every mornin' at sun-up, walkin' by here on his way to Needle Rock."

"Walkin' by here, Zeth?" said Red incredulously. "You shore you ain't been seein' things?"

"Nope! Shore as I'm sittin' here, every mornin' just 'fore sun-up he comes trudgin' by here 'bout a mile to the east."

Red leaned eagerly forward in his chair.

"What did he look like?"

"Huh?" Zeth gaped, scratched his head and looked puzzled. "I don't rightly know."

"Think hard, Zeth! I've got to know what he looked like!"

Zeth's brow furrowed and he puffed hard in short jerks on his pipe. Red and Little Beaver strained toward him, waiting. If Zeth could only remember!

"Sorry, Red," he said finally, shaking his head. "Can't remember a single thing about him, 'ceptin' he always walks like he's mighty tired. After all, sun isn't even up when I see him. You can't tell what a man looks like in the grey mornin' light a mile away."

Red frowned with disappointment, but quickly recovered himself. After all, he was at last on the right trail. A man *walking* back to Needle Rock just before sun-up every morning certainly invited investigation. In this cattle country, even the poorest man didn't walk places without a good reason. Everyone owned a horse; it was a necessity of life.

Needle Rock was only a couple of miles farther on. It loomed large and menacing, resembling somewhat the gruesome, medieval conception of a witch's playground. The needle-like pinnacles, eight in all, from which the rock got its name, pointed to the sky, ready, it seemed, to pierce anything that dropped upon them.

Taking their leave of the Todds, Red Ryder and Little Beaver slowly cantered toward their ominous goal. Though they watched it constantly, there was not a single sign of life. A lazy wind blew a fine flow of dust up against its jagged surface. As the dust hit the rock and traveled upward, finally arching out, it reminded Red of a lazy sea dashing against the rocks on the coast.

The sun burned fiercely, and the stored-up heat of the rock shimmered the air about it, making it seem as though the rock were swaying. It was unlikely that any man or animal peered down upon them as they approached. The heat was too great for anything living to stand it long.

This, of course, was an advantage to Red and Little

Beaver. Before the sun had traveled much farther across the heavens, they would be safely hiding in a cave—one that Red and Little Beaver had discovered by pure accident the year before.

Anxious to get out of the terrible sun, they spurred their foam-covered mounts over the last half mile and quickly made their way up a narrow natural path, out of the dazzling light. They blinked their eyes, totally blind for a moment in the comparatively dark shade of the rock. Finally, accustomed to it, they dismounted and led Thunder and the pony to a huge boulder.

Red leaned a shoulder to it, the rock teetered for a moment as though thinly balanced, then fell away, revealing a large opening. A cool rush of air hit them in the face and they smiled with relief.

"That sure feelum much good!" exclaimed Little Beaver.

"Ahhhhhh!" was all that Red Ryder could answer, spreading his arms so that the cool air swirled around his hot, sweating body.

They led in the cayuses. The animals neighed appreciatively, shook themselves, pawed the rock and hurried to the cool, subterranean spring bubbling in the center of the dirt floor.

The man and boy stripped off their clothes and dashed the cold water on their steaming bodies. It was cold and shocking—but oh, so good! They drank sparingly, knowing that violent cramps, and sometimes death, may result

Red Was Trapped in the Cave!

from overdrinking when the body has been overheated.

When Thunder was unsaddled and he and the pony were brushed down, the man and boy stretched out on the cool dry floor and slept. A hard night's work was ahead of them, and they weren't likely to get much "shut-eye," if any at all.

Red was a light sleeper. He sensed danger subconsciously, even before the slightest sound was made. He was wide awake in an instant, every nerve, every muscle, taut and ready for action.

When he sat up, his two six-shooters ready for business, snatched from their leather in a blur of speed as quickly as his eyes opened, there was nothing in the cave, the horses were quietly standing by the spring.

Red was puzzled for an instant—but for *only* an instant. A long slithering shadow fell across the mouth of the cave, then the leering head of a wolf edged into sight.

Red's guns spat lead. The head disappeared. Red lurched to his feet. He rushed toward the opening, but too late. There was a grinding sound and the heavy boulder fell back into place, completely covering the exit.

Red stopped in amazement. Little Beaver scurried to his side.

"What happened?" he asked, bewilderedly.

Red wordlessly flipped the guns into their holsters and threw himself against the rock. It wouldn't budge. Little Beaver lent his slight weight to a second attempt. Still nothing happened.

After several minutes of fruitless shoving, pushing and grunting, they slipped panting to the ground.

"What we do now?"

"We're trapped, Little Beaver!"

"Can't understand why rock move-um so easy before, an' now won't make-um budge," muttered the little Indian boy, shoving his fist beneath his chin.

"It's simple enough," mumbled Red. "The fulcrum that the boulder balances upon, runs crosswise. On the outside, we push with it—in here we're pushing against it."

"No one know where we are, so no one ever find us," muttered Little Beaver in a frightened voice.

"That's about the size of it, young 'un," answered Red, trying to make his tone light. "We're trapped good and proper!"

CHAPTER V

CAVE OF TERROR

The realization of what lay ahead, as they pressed their backs against the cold, unyielding rock, settled on their minds like a pall. At the far end of the room was a small corridor, leading they knew not where. Once they set foot in it, followed its winding course into the bowels of the earth, there was no telling where they would land. Cave corridors wind unpredictably, follow a mad, patternless course—slant cross and criss-cross each other until, within a short space of time, a wanderer is forever lost, doomed to a death of slow, maddening starvation in the suffocating, inky blackness.

Pressed against the boulder, there was always some hope. A stranger might pass—or perhaps Mrs. Lerner might decide to pay her long-deferred visit to Zeth Todd's wife. Quite accidentally she *might* choose the trail passing the boulder and hear their frantic tapping on the outside.

But such hopes were flimsy. A man of Red Ryder's fighting spirit did not wait passively for death. Such men take up the challenge—meet it halfway, driving on and on until the last instinct to live has departed.

Angry at his own carelessness for leaving himself and Little Beaver open to such a trap, Red Ryder jumped to his feet and felt his way through the blackness to the horses. They stood quietly near the bubbling spring, sensing their master's nearness.

Red reached out in the darkness, his hand closed over a fistful of the long silky mane of his beloved pinto, Thunder. He felt the horse's neck wrinkle as it turned toward him. Then the cool feel of its snout skimmed his cheek affectionately.

"I'm leavin' you for a little while, ol' fellow," he whispered into the pinto's ear. "And I ain't sure I'm comin' back. But if there's any way outa this place . . . Little Beaver an' me will find it and let you and the pony out pronto. So long, pal!"

Gently, he pushed the stretching head from him, knelt to the floor and felt for his saddle bag. He took from it his canteen, some dry biscuits and, on a second thought, took his lariat from the saddle horn. He could hear Little Beaver moving around, probably getting his own belongings.

"Just take your canteen and some jerk meat, Little Beaver. We're travelin' light."

"Little Beaver ready . . ."

"Okay, young 'un. Grab hold of my belt and let's get goin'."

The journey was one that neither of them could soon forget. The blackness was complete—so complete it seemed almost a thing of substance. They could not see two inches ahead. Every step had to be felt, tested, made certain. One false move might hurtle them into a bottomless abyss, or loosen a rock which would start a cave-in. No matter how careful they were, many times they stumbled, fell—cut themselves on the sharp rocks. Soon their clothes were in ribbons. Little Beaver's bare chest was wet with blood from a thousand scratches.

Time seemed to stand still. They had no conception of it, nor of how far they had traveled. All they knew was that they were horribly tired, aching and burning with pain. Every body fiber cried for rest, but something strong within forced them onward. Just ahead, it seemed to urge, around the next bend—soon, soon they would be out, looking up at the sky, across the plains, and into each other's eyes.

The cavern wall became slimy and damp; the rough floor, slippery under foot. Breaking the awful stillness, a dull roaring reached their ears. It grew louder as they progressed.

"Sound like river, Red Ryder."

"Yo're right!" agreed the cowboy, excitedly. "And if we can only get to it, we've got a good chance of breaking out of this hole!"

Eagerly they stumbled and slid forward. The rumbling of the water grew louder, and with it mounted the hope in their hearts. Feeling their way along the right hand wall, they came to a spot where the water seemed near—so near they had to shout to speak to each other.

"We're near it, Little Beaver," yelled Red. "Take it real

easy or we might fall in!"

"Um—um!" cried the little Indian, too excited to say more.

The crashing, tumbling roar of the water was deafening for a moment. But as the seconds passed, the roar diminished, became a distant rumble once again.

"Hold it," said Red, stopping.

They stood in an archway leading to another cavern.

"We passed up our spot back a piece. Take hold o' my hand. We're crossing to the other side and back trackin'."

Little Beaver fitted his small fingers into Red's long hard palm. Side by side, they skidded and stumbled across the treacherous floor to the opposite wall. Then, resuming their former position, Little Beaver clutching Red's belt, they headed back. Much to their relief, the roaring grew louder by the second. Again the sound reached a crescendo. The next step brought them to an opening in the wall.

Trembling with excitement, but suspicious of the treacherous ground, Red slid his hand down the wall and crouched to the floor. He stretched as far as he could to make sure there was no sudden drop off into the river. Solid, slimy rock met his inquisitive hands all the way.

"Get down and hold on to my boot," he ordered Little Beaver.

The boy, firm in his belief in Red Ryder, and Red's ability to get them out of this death trap, responded to the order without a word. Inch by inch, they crawled forward.

"Stop!" shouted Red, over the deafening roar.

He reached back and pulled Little Beaver up beside him. Little Beaver's trembling fingers felt the ledge, reached farther out and felt nothing. They were on a ridge alongside the river.

Grabbing Red's arm, he pulled the cowboy down so that his lips fitted into his ear.

"Which way river run? Opening should-um be downstream!"

Red moved his head so that he could shout into Little Beaver's ear. "Hold still, I'll let you know·in a minute."

Red reached around to the back of his belt and loosened his lariat. Uncoiling it, he played it out slowly. Suddenly, he felt it grow taut and pull to his right. His face, strained from the grueling demands of the journey, relaxed in a smile. Now he knew for certain, at least, that there *was* a way out—and it lay to the right!

With deft fingers, he looped one end of the lariat around Little Beaver's waist, and circled the rest around his own. Carefully turning to the right, he began to crawl on hands and knees. Little Beaver followed close at his heels.

A few feet farther on, Red's hand touched a wall, running along the side. He stretched his other arm out and felt the ledge with the tip of his fingers. He roughly calculated that the ledge was at least four feet wide, plenty of room for them to progress without too much danger.

Occasionally, the ledge narrowed to a couple of feet or less, hardly room to pass. Somehow, they managed to get by these danger spots without mishap. After a while, the river grew quieter, the ledge wider. They were able to get to their feet and walk standing up.

Suddenly, Red stopped, gazed straight ahead.

"Yip-YIPEEEEEEEEE!"

"Stars!" shouted Little Beaver.

Ahead of them, framed in a rugged archway, was a mantle of twinkling bright stars, stretched across the heavens and dipping into the horizon. The Milky Way had never before looked so good nor shone so beautifully.

They pushed toward their freedom with pounding hearts. When they were about one hundred feet from the arched entrance, the subterranean river took a sharp curve, dipped down and away, pursuing its ever dark, mysterious channel into the depths of the earth. For a moment, they stood at the bend and looked down at the faintly visible water, catching at this point faint reflections of the starlight outside, as it rushed by toward the black tunnel beyond. It seemed almost as though the river had felt their helplessness back there, called them to it with its stentorian roar, guided them to safety and freedom, and sent them on their way to the world above.

"I'll never forget this river," murmured Red Ryder softly. "It shore saved our lives."

Little Beaver nodded. "Heap good river."

They covered the remaining ground quickly, passing through a large cavern similar to the one they had entered in the afternoon. The sharp night air, when they reached the open, had a cold snap to it that chilled them to their bones. But it felt good! They were free!

Still their troubles were not over. They found themselves high up, close to the summit of one of the needle-like cliffs. The cliff was smooth and shining in the bright starlight as they looked down. Not a single foothold marred its side. Descent seemed impossible.

"Out o' the fryin' pan into the fire," muttered Red ruefully, taking note of the situation. "How in tarnation are we gonna get down now?"

"Red Ryder's lariat good and strong," suggested Little Beaver.

" 'Tain't long enough."

Red studied their position carefully, shook his head, then looked upward. A hopeful light came into his eye.

About twenty feet above, the cliff came to a peak. Continuing above the peak, was a narrow projection jutting upward like a bayonet from a rifle.

"Yore lariat idea might work yet, young 'un," opined Red, gathering the rope from around his waist and slipping the loop end off Little Beaver. "Stand back!"

The lariat loop whistled in an ever-widening circle, suddenly shot upwards toward the jutting rock, hovered for a second over its mark, then snugly settled down around it.

"Ah!" sighed Red, pulling the line tight. "That does it."

"Good shot," mumbled Little Beaver, shortly.

The difficult roping feat didn't amaze him one bit. He expected perfection from Red in such things. To him, the red-headed cowboy was like the Robin Hood of legend—infallible.

"You go first," ordered Red. He picked Little Beaver up, and held him over his head so the Indian boy would grasp the rope high up, thus having a shorter climb. "Don't hurry, be shore o' yore footin' and if anythin' happens, I'll be down here to catch you."

"Little Beaver ain't big baby. He only fall-um when rope bust-um," replied Little Beaver indignantly, and started up, hand over hand.

Red smiled to himself, but watched the boy's every move. Gaining the archway over the entrance, Little Beaver braced his feet against the wall, leaned back, held tightly to the rope and began to walk horizontally to the top. Red beamed with pride. The kid sure could take care of himself!

Red followed hurriedly and reached the pinnacle to find Little Beaver pointing excitedly below. Red groaned, and then began to chuckle. The amusing aspect of the situation took a firmer hold on him, and soon he was roaring uncontrollably with laughter. Little Beaver's high treble joined in and they laughed until their already aching sides, ached more.

The torturous, stumbling journey through the tunnel;

the hours of pain and bruises—all their horrible lost wanderings through the caverns of Needle Rock, had brought them to a point ten feet above the place where they had entered that afternoon!

Directly below them, still firmly planted against the entrance, was the huge boulder that had almost spelled their doom. Anyone else would probably have complained bitterly. But Red's bubbling sense of humor reacted mirthfully and saw it for the good joke that it was.

They let themselves down the opposite side in high spirits, pushed the boulder aside and whistled for their mounts. They weren't taking any chances of being trapped again.

Thunder and the little Indian pony whinnied loudly and galloped out to their masters. Little Beaver went inside to gather up Red's saddle, blanket and carbine, while Red stood guard. His sharp eyes, accustomed to the dense blackness of the cave, pierced the shadows of the comparatively bright night all about them. But all was still; there was no movement anywhere.

There was much to be done yet that night, and many hours had been lost. Red judged from the position of the stars that it was past midnight; he knew that the werewolf had been out stalking—killing. He had hoped to prevent another killing by hunting out and coming to grips with the creature when it left Needle Rock to carry out its bloody mission. But the creature had turned the tables; and left Red and Little Beaver to die a horrible death of starvation.

Now, however, Red mused that the tables were again turned. The creature thought them prisoners lost somewhere in the bowels of the earth. He would, therefore, return to Needle Rock by morning. High up on the rocks, Red and Little Beaver could watch his return, stalk him as he did his victims, then capture him in a lightning surprise attack. Perhaps—though it was tragic that another life had been sacrificed—perhaps it was best this way, and they would be certain to catch the quarry.

"Where we go now?" asked Little Beaver, as Red swung himself into the saddle.

"It's about four hours to sun-up, I reckon," said Red. "So we got time to mosey down and drop in on Mrs. Lerner in the valley. I got a hunch she's been one o' this werewolf's victims."

"If werewolf make home here," answered the little Indian, getting to his pony's back, "then he sure kill-um her first. Too bad," he sighed, shaking his head. "She one swell-um lady. Good cook too. Make good hot tamales."

Red smiled, then his face grew grave. Something had flashed into his mind—an awful picture that made him shudder.

"On second thought, I ain't so sure she's dead, Little Beaver. If what I'm thinkin's true, she'd probably be better off if she were. Leastwise, unless we can fix things up for her."

He touched spurs to Thunder's flanks and shot off down the sloping rock trail. Little Beaver urged his pony after him. His brow wrinkled in wonder at Red Ryder's strange words.

Rounding a large rock, the two riders saw the house set in the middle of about one hundred acres of level land. Needle Rock surrounded it on all sides like a grim fortress. The house was bathed in moonlight and strangely enough, at this late hour, a light burned in the window.

"Come on, Little Beaver," shouted Red.

Their sure-footed animals picked their way down the narrow gorge, reached the ground and galloped toward the house. When they were about a hundred yards away, they reined in and came to a stop.

"Halooo there!" yelled Red. "Don't be frightened, Mrs. Lerner. It's only Red Ryder and Little Beaver."

He took the precaution of warning her because he knew that in dangerous times like these, the occupants of the house might follow the old frontier axiom: "Shoot first and ask questions afterward."

Red and Little Beaver had no hankering to court lead.

A few seconds after he shouted his warning, the door of the house flew open, and they could see a woman's figure outlined in the doorway.

"Red Ryder! . . . Red Ryder! Is it *really* you?" her voice sounded hysterical.

"Yes'm. Me an' little Beaver."

They galloped up and dismounted in front of Rita

Lerner. For a moment, they stood aghast, hardly able to believe their eyes. This young woman whom they had seen but a few short months before, gay, beautiful and light-hearted with zest for life, had completely changed.

Tortured, harrowed eyes gazed at them out of a face gaunt from privation—she had clearly been having a very hard time. Her clothes were torn and dirty; her hair hung matted and stringy over her shoulders; her face was disfigured with ugly scratches.

Red could not conceal the shock her appearance gave him. His eyes widened, his jaw dropped—he stood speechless.

"Don't look at me that way!" screeched Rita Lerner, covering her face.

"I'm—I'm sorry, Mrs. Lerner," Red apologized, stepping toward her, filled with shame for his rudeness. "Powerful sorry—I just didn't know what to make of—"

"Of me?" cried the miserable woman. "Of what I look like? Look at me! Stare at me! I might as well be dead!" Her hands pressed tightly against her grimy, swollen face, her shoulders convulsed; she laughed and cried hysterically.

"Easy there, Mrs. Lerner. Everything's going to be all right now," said Red softly.

He took her arm and led her toward the house. What he saw shocked his senses more than his first sight of Rita Lerner.

Furniture lay strewn about the floor, smashed. Shreds

of cloth and paper torn by maniacal hands littered the place like a city street after a parade; bones, with vestiges of red, raw meat still clinging to them, lay where they were thrown. In a corner, a half devoured cow, feasted upon by a horde of flies, filled the room with a horrible stench.

Red took it all in at a single glance and automatically recoiled. Rita Lerner suddenly became still. She watched the disgust on Red's face and her eyes seemed to start from her head. She began to giggle—all sense and reason gone.

Not taking her eyes from Red, she moved backward to the center of the room, kicked away some of the cluttered mess on the floor, bent down to tug at an iron ring. With the super strength of the mad, she pulled the trap door open, and shrieking with delight, pointed down into the dark cavity below.

"Look, look! Hah, hah, hah, hah, hah!" Her crazy laugh mounted and fell, broken by gasping sobs.

Red came toward her. Little Beaver waited fearfully at the door, his coal-black eyes fastened pitifully upon the insane woman. It was hard for him to understand that this was the same Mrs. Lerner who, with her young husband, had been so cheerful and kind.

Red Ryder stared into the cavity. The single oil lamp hardly reached the space below, and all he could see were faint blobs of white. Reaching up, he took the lamp from its hook and held it down below the floor level.

His body tensed and a low horrified moan escaped his lips. He straightened up and closed his eyes for an instant, to open them and gaze accusingly at the hysterical woman. The steady, unwavering look had a quieting effect upon her. Sanity returned to her eyes and her laughter reduced to hard sobs.

"No, Red Ryder! No—not me!"

"Who then?"

Her face clouded over and she turned away, burying her face in her hands again.

"Who then?" Red's tone was quiet, insistent, and there was no mistaking its intensity. "Who killed the people whose skeletons are below?"

She turned slowly back to him. Tears welled from her eyes, though her sobbing had ceased. There was a certain defiance in her attitude as she looked at him. Something inside had called back her sanity, geared her mind to alertness.

"I don't know, Red," she replied quietly.

Red studied her face, his steel grey eyes narrowed to gleaming slits.

"I'm sorry, Ma'am, but yo're lyin' to me."

Rita Lerner's eyes dropped, but she made no answer.

"Can't you see, I've got to know who it is," Red said urgently. "People are bein' killed every night by this—this fiend. Innocent people, Mrs. Lerner—people who are yore friends an' mine."

"I don't know, I tell you—*I don't know!*"

Red could not help feeling pity for the woman. Whatever her secret was, it lay close to her heart. He could see that a constant battle waged within her—whether to reveal or continue to protect and suffer. Despite all that she had been through—all that she knew—she was still loyal to whatever it was. If all that had happened had not broken down her loyalty, Red realized that words and threats were useless.

"You win, Ma'am. I reckon me an' Little Beaver can work this thing out by ourselves," he said heavily. "Little Beaver an' me is gonna take a look around in the basement an' see if we can identify any o' the people down there."

Rita Lerner nodded slowly. "Please do," she answered. "I want their families to know what happened to them."

Red looked at her queerly, shrugged his shoulders and motioned Little Beaver to come with him. The tiny Indian pinched his nose to kill the stench of the rotting steer and minced into the room.

They were about to descend the stairs when Rita Lerner took the lamp from Red's hand.

"Wait, I'll go along and tell you who each one is."

Red's stern face softened. "Thank you, Ma'am."

Crash!

The tinkle of broken glass. Darkness!

Red wheeled in a rocking crouch. Almost in the fraction of the second that the light snuffed out, Red's six-shooters were clear of their holsters, cocked and sweeping a wide circle, blazing orange jets of flame at the unseen target.

A howl rose in the room. Red saw a shadow, but, before he was sure of it, it had disappeared. He strained his eyes to pierce the dark and kept his guns roaring. Behind him he heard a muffled scream, a yelp from Little Beaver, then the bump of bodies rolling down a flight of stairs.

He pivoted fast, but held his fire, fearful that he might hit Little Beaver and Mrs. Lerner. The loud bang of the trapdoor falling into place startled him and sent little nerve warnings up and down his spine.

The blood pounded in his temples and a keen, exultant sense overcame him as he waited the attack that was sure to come.

Man or beast? Natural or supernatural? What was this thing that was about to vent its mad fury on Red Ryder? His muscles tensed, eager and ready to go into action.

The room was deathly still. Red held his breath and strained his ears for the slightest sound to betray the whereabouts of his adversary. Crouched low as he was, he felt confident that the werewolf was also searching for him, holding its breath against discovery.

The seconds dragged by. Red's lungs were bursting, but to exhale would be fatal. Finally, when it was no longer possible to hold it in, a sound reached his ears to his left, a little behind him.

He started to pivot, but something heavy crashed down

on his wrists. His hands went numb and he heard his
two guns crash to the floor. The next instant, a fury of
blows rained down upon him. The numbness crept up
his arms and his fists refused to double. Backing away,
giving ground, he protected himself as best he could.
Luckily the door was behind him, and he backed into
the open.

The werewolf followed, howling and clawing and
beating. Once in the open, Red could see the figure plainly. Wise in the knowledge of a fighter, he watched the
talon-like feet, waiting for a chance to get the deadly
killer off balance.

Suddenly, he saw his chance. The werewolf had stepped back and for an instant was rocking on his heels.
Red's muscles reacted—one hundred and ninety pounds
of bone, muscle and grit rammed into the snarling beast's
midsection. The piercing howl cut off like an alarm
clock. The gnarled body shot backward and slammed
against the cabin wall.

Red lowered his head and charged in, his arms hanging
loosely at his sides. He was certain that if he had their
use, he could finish the beast off instantly. But no matter
how great the disadvantage, how many the obstacles,
Red's credo never allowed him to stop fighting as long
as breath and life were in his body.

Using his head as a battering ram, Red hurtled forward with every ounce of reserve strength he could muster. It was his only chance and he knew it. He closed his

eyes for the impact.

Bang!

The werewolf stood over Red howling and beating its chest triumphantly. At the last moment, he had side-stepped and Red had crashed head-on into the wall.

Unconscious, he lay at the feet of the bloodthirsty, howling beast!

CHAPTER VI

AMONG THE SKELETONS

The wolf cry reverberated against the ashen cliffs of Needle Rock, sounding defiance and hate. The dripping jowls of the werewolf spread wide and pointed skyward as though trying to lift its voice over the confines of the valley out into the world to let people know that he had conquered their champion.

Little Beaver, locked beneath the floor, strained against the trap door. He listened to the awful cry of victory with unbelieving ears.

"No! . . . No!" he cried and beat his fists against the unyielding wood.

Rita Lerner lay at the bottom of the stairs, stretched out just as she had fallen. Her eyes, wide open, stared into the dark and she too heard the cry. Her body quivered at the sound and then she lay perfectly still. Little Beaver's cries and the pounding of his fists brought a bitter smile to her lips.

"Save your strength, Little Beaver, or you will die more quickly," she muttered in a toneless voice. "Now that Red Ryder is dead, you will become one of these skeletons."

"Red Ryder not dead . . . Not DEAD!" screamed the small Indian boy, stumbling down the steps.

"What else? The werewolf cries with victory. I have heard it many times before."

"Red Ryder alive!" insisted Little Beaver. "You see . . . You see!"

But even as he spoke, doubt gnawed at his mind. He tried to shake it off, remembering the strength and invincibility of Red Ryder in other battles, where Red had overcome far greater odds than were now against him.

The unceasing cry taunted him—slowly killed his hopes. He couldn't believe it! Red Ryder couldn't be dead —just couldn't be! And as he tried to wish and think Red Ryder alive, another memory stirred in him; the time he had seen his own father thrown from a bucking bronco, dashed to the earth and trampled to death by the enraged beast.

It was through this terrible tragedy that he had met Red Ryder; while he stood looking helplessly down at his father's broken, twisted body, the rangy cowboy had suddenly come riding over the hill. Calmly, he had taken in the situation at a glance; comforted the dumbfounded, grief-stricken boy; and, after the burial, taken him away without a word, to watch over and adopt him as his own.

The same empty, surprised, hurt feeling that gripped him in the pit of his stomach during those first moments when he gazed down at the broken, twisted body of his parent, hit him again as he sank to the steps and buried his head in his hands. Dry sobs racked his lungs and his little fists clenched tightly, forced against his mouth to cover the sound.

"If Red Ryder dead—Little Beaver wantum die too."

"It isn't easy, little one," came the mournful voice of Rita Lerner from the dark below. "No matter how much you want to die—you want to live more. But the werewolf gives no choice—you will die, little one, soon—soon!"

As the last word fell from her lips, the howling stopped. An ominous silence followed for several minutes, and Little Beaver found himself holding his breath. Then he heard a slight rustle as Rita Lerner stirred herself and sat up.

"He has gone to his lair!" she said in a voice that hissed. "He is leaving me to die here with you."

Little Beaver trembled and rose on the steps. Some instinct warned him to prepare for something. He unslung his bow from his back, fitted the thong into its notch; tested the pull of the weapon; drew an arrow and nocked it.

The soft pad of bare feet and the slight scratch of long claws on the floor above reached his ears. He drew back the bowstring and held the arrow steady, aimed at the trap door, dead center. The door lifted. Little Beaver took a step upward and tensed.

The sound of labored breathing reached his ears as the door opened all the way. He was set—ready to let fly his arrow—but there was nothing to shoot at.

Suddenly, two arms reached over the opening from

the side, holding a long limp figure. A short gasp of delight broke from Little Beaver's lips, and he lowered his bow.

Red Ryder!

The long lanky figure was unmistakable; the flat crowned, broad-brimmed hat hanging from his neck by its chin strap definitely identified him.

"Li-tt-le Beav—," groaned an all too familiar voice, and Little Beaver felt a new surge of life running through him at its sound.

Red Ryder was alive! He was hurt—but alive! From now on it was up to Little Beaver. Now that Red was temporarily out of the picture, he knew that escape for the cowboy and Mrs. Lerner was entirely dependent upon him.

In another second, Red's limp body would come tumbling down the stairs. It would be too late then. He had to act immediately.

With the thought, he sprang into action, cleared the few steps to the top and darted across the cabin floor out into the first grey of dawn; paused for a second outside of the door, turning swiftly to find his Indian pony. He spotted it at the side of the house, where it grazed with Red's pinto, Thunder.

A loud enraged howl came from inside the house. The sound of a body thumping down the stairs and the bang of the trap door closing, reached his ears; then the hard pounding of heavy bare feet across the floor toward the door.

Horrible fright choked him as he scuttled across the ground to his pony. He could sense the lightning approach of the werewolf behind him, and knew that his chances of reaching his mount and making an escape were slim.

But fright gave him that extra burst of strength and speed needed. Somehow, he was across the ground, leaping into the air, gripping the pony's sides with his knees and kicking his moccasined feet into its flanks.

The sensitive animal sprang from a standstill and strained every muscle in response to its master's urging. Little Beaver lay high along its neck, his mouth touching the pointed ear, murmuring frightened encouragement to it in his native tongue.

The sharp, cold wind felt good on his fevered face as the pony carried him across the valley. Far behind, the howl of the wolf faded into the distance and soon stopped all together. Little Beaver glanced over his shoulder to see if perhaps the beast followed him. If the beast had the speed of a real wolf, Little Beaver knew that he would never get beyond the treacherous confines of Needle Rock.

The sight that greeted his eye when he turned, made him cry with relief. The werewolf had given up the chase after a few hundred yards, and stood framed in the first vertical rays of the sun, shaking his fists at the Indian boy. Little Beaver didn't know whether he actually saw it, or whether it was just imagination, but little jets of fire seemed to spring from the eyes of the beast which walked upright like a man but had the head of a wolf.

The trip through the narrow passes of Needle Rock was made easier by the mounting sunlight. Little Beaver made good time and galloped down the rocky slope on the far side, as the first horizontal rays drenched the plain. A silvery mist arose from the dew-drenched earth —promise of a sizzling hot day. In a few minutes, as though an invisible egg-beater was revolving, the mist whirled higher and higher, like cotton candy on a stick, and soon disappeared altogether.

The Indian pony was breathing heavily and foam drenched its sleek hide, but it did not slacken speed for a single instant. Little Beaver headed toward Zeth Todd's ranch house where welcome smoke poured from the chimney. At this sign of peaceful life, Little Beaver felt, for the first time since Red and he had left the same house the previous afternoon, a feeling of security.

The sound of the pony's pounding hooves brought the entire family to the door. As Little Beaver leaped from his pony's back, they rushed toward him.

"Little Beaver! What in the dickens—?"

Zeth Todd's eyes gaped in astonishment at the sight of the little Indian. His bare body was torn, scratched and a mass of bloody welts; his round intense face, dirty with sweat, grime and smeared blood. So preoccupied had Red and Little Beaver been after they had escaped from the cave, that they had not thought to bathe the cuts and wounds from the sharp cave rocks.

"Me all right!" shouted Little Beaver. "Mrs. Lerner and Red Ryder in danger. Prisoners of werewolf!"

Zeth and Mrs. Todd started in fright; Mrs. Todd automatically clutched her son Danny to her side.

"How'd you escape?" asked Zeth.

"No time to talk now! Gotta ride gettum posse an' go back Needle Rock. You gottum fresh horse for me? Pony tired."

Little Beaver stamped impatiently in front of them.

Zeth, overcoming his surprise at seeing the Indian boy's battered condition, took command of the situation.

"Yo're stayin' here an' lettin' Mrs. Todd fix up those wounds on yore body," he said, and started toward the stable. "I'll ride for the posse."

Little Beaver trotted at his heels, looking doubtful. "Me better ride with you."

"No need for that. Get yoreself fixed up an' get a good meal inside you. We'll pick you up on the way back."

Still not quite decided, Little Beaver stood inside the stable watching Zeth Todd saddle a low, fast little mustang, which, though not much to look at, showed the power and stability which was its heritage.

"You hurry back with posse?" asked Little Beaver.

"Be back here 'fore noon. Don't you worry."

Todd mounted his horse. The animal reared half way up on its hind legs and sprang away, its short muscular legs eating up the ground effortlessly.

Little Beaver watched it from the stable door until it was only a speck and a cloud of dust. He then walked slowly toward the house. For the first time, he felt the weariness that the arduous demands of the night had caused; sharp stinging pain from the cuts and bruises on his body suddenly made him wince. Danny Todd ran to him and helped him into the house, where Mrs. Todd already had some hot water ready to wash his wounds.

When the wounds were clean, Little Beaver took his little herb sack from his belt and showed Mrs. Todd how to apply the salves. The sting soon went away and Little Beaver felt refreshed, relaxed, and ravenously hungry.

The cure for that too was ready, and Little Beaver dug into a juicy steak garnished with crisp home-fried potatoes, and flaky home-made bread and butter. Between eager bites, he gulped down a pitcher of cold milk. When he was finished, he felt his stomach comfortably, smiled drowsily at hostess and son, and fell asleep.

The thunderous sound of many hooves awakened him several hours later. Grabbing his bow and arrows from a chair beside the bunk where Mrs. Todd had carried him, he leaped to his feet and rushed outside. Wrapped in a cloud of dust, the posse of ranchers were pulling up in front of the house. When the dust swirls had cleared, Little Beaver was able to pick out familiar faces: "Harky" Walters, Ted Lynch, Sam Locke and others. Sheriff Parks and his son, Lem, led the posse, and for this Little Beaver

Trapped in the Cellar

was glad.

Almost as he came out of the door, Danny Todd was leading his Indian pony around the corner from the stables. Little Beaver vaulted on its back and without a word, took the lead, the posse following him.

As the early morning mist had promised, the day turned into an inferno. The sun beat down upon the thundering riders, burning through their thick flannel shirts. Little Beaver's bare body, tender from the scratches and wounds, soon was red and swelling, the fresh scabs cracking and little jets of blood oozing from the crevices.

They reached Needle Rock and started up the narrow gorge between two pinnacles, single file. They passed the cave entrance, which no longer looked tempting to Little Beaver, and moved quickly toward the gorge leading into the valley. They rounded the last rock, shielding the valley from sight, and a cry of alarm broke from Little Beaver's lips.

The farmhouse was a mass of sky-reaching flames. Small fires were starting in the fields from the flying embers, and were rapidly spreading.

"Hurry!" cried Little Beaver, forcing his pony down the slope. "Red Ryder and Mrs. Lerner under house!"

There were startled cries from the men, and the next instant they followed Little Beaver down the treacherous slope. As they rode, Sheriff Parks was uncoiling his lariat and forming a plan. Though he hadn't had a chance to talk to the Indian boy, he realized that the werewolf had locked Red Ryder and Mrs. Lerner in the cellar.

There was only one way to get them out before the house burned down and the embers cooled over their bones!

Dodging their horses between the scattered flame spots in the field, the posse was soon near the house. The heat was so intense that the horses reared on their haunches, refusing to go nearer. As a man, the posse leaped to the ground and ran toward the house, holding arms in front of faces to ward off the direct heat.

Sheriff Parks swung his lariat as he ran, looking for a target. Part of the roof had fallen in and a beam stuck out invitingly. He stopped and let go the rope. It went true to its mark, hitching fast on the beam. The Sheriff ran back to his horse and sprang into the saddle.

The other men stopped and fell back a little, understanding what he was doing. His horse leaped forward, straining, bucking, leaping. The wall began to give.

Lem Parks and Little Beaver quickly followed his plan and ran around to opposite sides, leading their cayuses, and unfurling their lariats. Both picked out projecting beams and let fly their separate ropes. Little Beaver's rope fell short, but Zeth Todd instantly stepped in, spinning his own lariat. It hit the beam and choked around it. He vaulted to his horse's back. The animal lowered its head, digging its hooves into the ground, muscles swelling and straining.

Lem Parks, meanwhile, had hit his mark and his wall

was giving rapidly. Sheriff Parks tugging the front wall, felt the strain suddenly ease, his horse move forward. The wall dragged on the ground, away from the foundations.

With one wall gone, the other cowboys had a chance to shoot their ropes into the room and pull out the fallen roof. In quick succession, walls two and three gave and were pulled out of the way.

Little Beaver meantime loosened the saddle of one of the posse horses, jerked off the saddle blanket. Wrapping it securely around him, so that no part of his body was exposed, he started toward the house. By the time he reached the place where the door had been, the walls were down and the center of the room cleared of the roof. The smell of burned meat reached his nostrils and he saw over in the corner the carcass of the steer that had fouled the air the night before. Now it was charred black.

Without hesitating a moment, he ran to the trap door. The terrific floor heat blistered the bottoms of his feet. He reached out to grab the iron ring, but pulled back quickly—it was red hot!

Muttering with irritation, he cast about for something to use as a holder. Every bit of metal in the room was glowing; too hot to handle. Heedless of the tiny licks of flame leaping around him, he whipped the blanket from his body and threw it over the ring. A thin puff of smoke immediately snuffed from underneath as the wool caught fire. Little Beaver grabbed the ring and, even under the several layers of the blanket, he could feel it burning his hand.

He tugged and strained, but the door would not budge. Then he realized that in his eagerness, he had forgotten to shoot the wedge that kept it tightly shut. The wedge formed a lump underneath the blanket and Little Beaver kicked at it with his foot, sliding it out of its bracket.

Zeth Todd again sprang to his side, reached down to grab the ring.

"Ring hot!" shouted Little Beaver in a voice cracked and choking from the smoke. "Use-um fresh part blanket where ring not burned through!"

"Thanks for the warnin', youngster."

Zeth pulled the blanket over and grasped at the ring beneath. The veins in his neck swelled as he strained to pull open the door. Suddenly, it gave with a groan. Little Beaver crouched low to peer inside.

A cloud of smoke swirled up, clouding everything below.

"Red Ryder!" screeched the little Indian, plunging down into the grey black cloud.

"Over here, Little Beaver," replied a weak, strained voice.

Little Beaver fought his way through the swirling fog down the steps toward the spot where he had heard the voice. He could hear footsteps on the stairs following him. Trying to pick his way, he stumbled and fell flat atop a skeleton. The dried bones rattled and cracked under his weight. Letting out a startled screech, he leaped to his feet and backed away.

With the rush of fresh air forcing out the smoke, the atmosphere began to clear. Over in a far corner, he saw two vague shadows—one tall, the other short. A swirl of smoke blocked his vision, but he made for the spot hurriedly.

He stopped short as the last dense bank of smoke shot up and away toward the trap door. There, two feet in front of him, was Red Ryder, swaying forward. In his arms he carried the still form of Rita Lerner.

"Hiya, young 'un?"

"Red Ryder—*safe!*"

The little Indian boy felt himself going weak all over and unashamed tears streamed from his eyes. In a happy daze, he felt someone brush past and saw Red Ryder collapse against him.

Someone else came, took Rita Lerner's limp body from Red's arms and carried her out. Then—and Little Beaver cared no longer—everything went black.

He regained consciousness some time later, to find himself lying in the welcome shade of a sprawling cottonwood. Red Ryder bent anxiously over him. His blistered little lips cracked into a painful smile as he looked into Red's eyes.

"We foolum werewolf again—yes, Red Ryder?"

The rangy cowboy swallowed hard, opened his mouth to answer, but only smiled and nodded. His eyes blinked and were unusually misty. His strong fingers gently gripped Little Beaver's arm, and the Indian knew what he was trying to say.

There was a relieved smile on all the anxious faces that looked down upon him. Little Beaver smiled back at these men who were his friends, though the effort was painful.

Sheriff Parks crouched across from Red and said:

"We gotta get you back to town an' let ole Doc Bradford take care o' those burns and wounds, Little Beaver. Feel strong enough to travel?"

"Little Beaver no needum white doctor," replied the Indian boy, sitting up and fumbling at his belt. "Me gottum medicine here."

"All the same—" the sheriff began.

"Let him be," interrupted Red. "I don't know what that stuff is he's got in that little sack o' his, but it's shore pow'ful stuff. I been treated with it and I know!"

In a little while, with Red's help, Little Beaver was smeared with the greenish substance and looked like a case of walking green measles.

Miraculously, Red and Rita Lerner had escaped without a single burn. Just before the trap door had been opened, the woman had fainted, overcome by the smoke, but upon reaching fresh air, she had quickly recovered.

"Where is Mrs. Lerner now?" asked Lem Parks, twisting his head about.

"I saw her lyin' down under that tree over there a few

minutes ago," volunteered "Harky" Walters, pointing to a lone pine on the far side of the smouldering embers.

"She ain't there now!"

They searched for her, calling her name. There was no answer. Red wrinkled his brow and narrowed his eyes, sweeping them over the valley. Something moved across a scorched spot in the wheat field. In two bounds he was in Thunder's saddle, streaking toward it.

The posse scrambled for their horses and shot after him. Little Beaver, stiff and sore, slowly climbed upon his mount and followed in their wake.

Reaching the scorched, bare spot in the field, Red reined in and studied the flow of the wheat. His eye fell on a trail of broken stalks. Dismounting, he waved the others to stand back.

Hitching his holsters around to the front, he walked into the wheat, his sensitive fingers hovering over the inlaid mahogany gun butts. The wheat swished against his hips as he moved through it, following a straight trail of broken stalks. He kept his eyes glued ahead for the slightest movement. For an instant he raised them to try to determine where the trail might be leading. A couple of hundred feet ahead, in the shadow of Needle Rock, was a high, big-branched elm tree, heavy with foliage and straining under the added burden of tentacle-like creepers.

Unless the trail veered sharply, it was heading straight for that point. As he moved cautiously forward, Red tried to figure out why Rita Lerner should suddenly disappear. There could be only one answer: the werewolf had seen her lying under the pine tree unwatched, and had kidnapped her. If this were true, he could only meet the beast in one way—*with bare fists!* The risk of using his guns was too great.

Though he was the fastest and truest gun master in the southwest, Red Ryder wasn't foolhardy enough not to realize that a wild bullet might hit the wrong target.

With keen remembrance of the hammer-like fists that had battered him mercilessly the night before, Red Ryder moved steadily forward. Though he still felt pain in his wrists, he felt equal to coping with the beast.

A few strides ahead, the tree loomed darkly. The foliage and creepers covered it so well, that only when Red was right on top of it did he see the small treehouse on the lower limbs, but high off the ground.

He stopped just outside the curtain of creepers, his head tilted slightly upward, his eyes searching out the treehouse. The part of the platform within his view was empty, but Red had the feeling that eyes were watching him from up there.

He reached out, tugged at the creepers and felt they were strong—capable of bearing his weight. It was the only way for him to get up. The rope ladder had been pulled up, out of reach.

Choosing a line of ascent along the strongest gnarled creepers, he started to climb, keeping his eyes for the most part on the treehouse. When he was halfway up, he saw a movement in the back and paused; the blood throbbed in his temples. Then a weird form separated from the shadows, stalked to the edge of the platform, and glared silently down at Red whose hand had dropped to his gun.

The awful figure was tall, broad and massively built; long, hairy arms with unbelievably long nails protruded from a shaggy wolf pelt, loosely thrown over the creature's otherwise naked body. An evil-looking wolf's head stared stoically down at Red. It was the most formidable creature Red had ever seen—and yet, as it stood there, it seemed almost pitiful in its ugliness.

"I wouldn't come any closer, if I was you. If you do, I'm gonna have to kill ya," said a hoarse voice.

Red started in surprise, almost losing his hold on the creeper, at the sound of the grotesque voice. Somehow, he had not connected anything but a horrible blood-curdling howl with this creature; the sound of the rather high-pitched voice unnerved him for a moment.

"You'll try, anyway," replied the redhead, coolly, resuming his climb.

"Get down . . . I'm warnin' ya!"

Red continued upward.

As Red got closer, the enraged creature crouched low, fists doubled, his breath coming in hard, uneven pants. Red's hand dipped down and out—his six-shooter came up aiming right between the werewolf's eyes.

The werewolf flattened himself on the floor out of Red's range and crawled back into the house. Red quickly pulled himself up until he was even with the floor, swung himself inside the creepers and leaped.

While he was still in mid-air the monster came charging out at him. Red's fist was swinging in a powerful uppercut even as his foot touched the floor. He "connected" and the wolf head snapped up. For a second, Red glimpsed a face beneath the head!

Whatever it was, then, was not a werewolf at all, as he had guessed—but a man *masquerading,* a man in wolf's clothing.

The smashing blow which Red had landed had by no means finished the monster. His powerful arms became a pair of flaying sledge hammers, beating into Red's face, arms and body. Red rushed inside the blows, locking his arms about the body. The pounding continued on his back, his head; dancing lights crowded before Red's eyes.

Squirming his shoulder into the "werewolf's" solar plexis, and driving forward with his legs, he forced the fight away from the edge of the floor. Then bringing his arms around to the front he drove short, piston-like blows into the midriff, keeping his head low, couched on the creature's chest.

As his blows gained more weight, he felt the other weakening. The beating on his back stopped and instead the gigantic paws clawed for a hold around Red's body. Red squirmed, dancing lightly on his feet, moving up and down, from one side to the other, always keeping his fists hammering away.

It was getting easier by the moment and Red felt victory close at hand. The creature retreated now, moving inside the house. His cries of pain shook the thin walls. Red followed him, crossing the threshold of the door. He felt the body suddenly stiffen—the huge arms once again clawed for a hold around Red's body. Red tried to squirm out of it, but his hip smacked up against the door. Wedged in, unable to use the squirming tactics he had applied so advantageously, Red saw that unless he could break away, the powerful arms would gain their hold around his body.

Drawing both fists back, he was about to drive them home with every ounce of strength he could muster when suddenly, his legs shot out from under him; the cruel arms had gained their hold, and in an instant the tide of battle had turned.

Red found himself floundering in an upside-down position, faced outward, away from the man's body. In this clumsy posture it was impossible to use his fists, practically impossible to do anything. Desperately, he caught hold of the solid arms, digging his nails into the flesh, pressing with all his might. The grip only tightened. The creature started to stagger forward toward the edge.

Twisting and kicking, Red felt his boot heels crash against the wolf head, but the blows were ineffective since the wolf mask acted as a shield as well as a disguise. In a few stumbling strides, his mad captor gained the edge of the flooring. For one awful second, Red hung suspended, gazing down backward at the hard, knotty exposed roots below.

Then the arms released their hold with a downward shove. Red bulleted toward the ground head-first!

CHAPTER VII

UNMASKED!

When Red looked down and saw the knotted roots below him, he knew what was to come. When the arms released their hold, he tensed his muscles and bent his head and body upward as far as possible. The hard downward shove came as a surprise, but his new position enabled him to act fast enough to overcome it.

Kicking his legs downward and flaying upward with his arms as he sped through the air, he completely righted himself and landed on his feet in a crouched position, but off balance. He fell against the tree, jarred and dazed.

On the other side, he heard a thud and then the sound of running feet. Crawling on hands and knees, he made his way around the tree trunk and saw the wolf-man diving behind a boulder at the foot of Needle Rock.

Red's fingers dipped for his guns, but came away empty. They had slipped from their holsters when he had been upside down. There was no time to fetch them. Furthermore, he had an idea that Rita Lerner was probably still up there and had hidden them.

Getting to his feet, Red shook his head to clear the cobwebs, vaulted through the creepers and ran toward the rock behind which he had seen the man disappear.

While running, he raised his head and uttered the high, piercing yell of the coyote. An answering call came in an instant, and far behind him he heard the pounding of horses' hooves.

The posse would see his path through the wheat stalks and follow him into the crevices winding through Needle Rock. He was confident Little Beaver could then follow his trail.

Reaching the boulder, he moved cautiously around it —but found nothing on the other side. An extremely narrow crevice cut through the cliff directly behind the boulder. It was the only possible path the wolf-man could have followed without being seen by Red.

Squeezing through the narrow entrance, Red's eyes lit up as he saw fur hairs sticking to the rock where they had been scraped off. The crevice widened a bit after the first few feet. By keeping his hands touching the sides so he wouldn't trip, Red was able to trot through the many turns and twists, and keep a close watch on what lay ahead.

When he looked up, it was because a spray of fine dirt and tiny pebbles had dropped to the ground just ahead of him. The wolf-man had left the crevice path and was climbing up the steep side with the agility of a mountain goat.

Red started to follow, but thought better of the idea when he spied the end of the crevice just ahead. He could cut the wolf-man off by gaining the additional forward ground and climbing at a lower point. If the killer should retreat, Red figured, he would fall into the arms of the posse. One way or the other—there was no escape for him.

Covering the ground quickly, Red left the path and came to a point where the walls veered down sharply. It wasn't often that breaks came Red's way to make his tasks easier, but before him for once was the answer to his prayers. A natural rock formation of steps led directly up to the point where the wolf-man would have to land when he jumped from the ledge above.

Red took the steps two at a time and threw himself underneath the overhanging ledge out of sight. He had not long to wait. He heard bare feet padding against the rock, then saw a shadow fall across the shelf in front of him. The next instant, the wolf-pelted figure landed a few feet ahead in a shock-breaking crouch.

Red started forward.

"Behind you!" he shouted, giving fair warning to the monster.

The wolf-man whirled. Behind the wolf mask, stark astonishment blazed from his eyes. Red lunged, meeting the maddened specimen of humanity for the first time on equal footing.

He sidestepped, catching Red with a staggering uppercut. Red fell back but the force of the blow only served to send his fighting blood coursing into every nerve and muscle of his body.

The wolf-man, thinking he had gained the advantage,

stepped in ready to finish it up quickly. Before his arms could pull back, fists with the kick of dynamite beat his head, arms and body without letting him land a single blow. He gave ground, floundering helplessly, trying to cover up. A torturing blow landed squarely in his solar plexus—he doubled up and howled with pain. Red shot a sweeping right underneath the wolf-head snout.

The mask flew off! Red's left was coming down for the knockout blow, but his eyes had finally seen the reason why the miserable man wore the wolf head and somehow he managed to stop his fist so that it landed harmlessly.

The man sank to the ground, all fight gone out of him, moaning and covering his face. Red stood over him, feeling sick inside. The horrible face—or the remains of a face—was the most nauseating thing Red had ever seen.

"Who are you?" he cried, swallowing hard.

"Don't ask me! . . . Please don't ask me!" moaned the beaten figure. "Pity me and let me be."

Red kept his eyes on the disfigured man, wary that he might make another break for freedom. He wet his dry lips with his tongue.

"I think I know who you are."

The moaning stopped, the face started to lift, but at sight of Red's horrified look, the man lowered it, hiding it behind his arms.

"If you know, keep it to yourself—I beg of you!"

"It's too late for that," Red answered, catching sight of

the posse out of the corner of his eye as it broke over a
ridge to the left. "You gotta pay for a lotta killin's. You
never showed them no mercy, so you can't be expectin'
none from us."

The posse left their horses in the canyon below and
scrambled up the slope on the opposite side.

"Before they come, hand me my mask," pleaded the
man. "I can't let them see me this way—*please!*"

"You hid behind that mask for the last time," said
Red, reaching into his pocket and pulling out a bandana.
"But you can wrap this 'round your face if you want
to." He dropped the cloth to the ground.

Eagerly, the man clutched it and tied it around his
face, just leaving the eyes free. "Thanks," he breathed,
and looked up at Red with eyes that seemed short of
boiling, edging between madness and sanity.

Sheriff Parks was the first to reach the shelf and hurry toward Red and his captive.

"You got him, Red! You got the yellow-livered, crawlin' varmint!" he shouted, gazing down at the man with
hate and scorn. "Who is it?"

The others rushed up, guns drawn and leveled at the
cowering figure on the ground.

"Who is it?" they chorused.

"Let's get a rope an' string him up!" someone shouted.

They pushed forward eagerly, reaching out to grab
him. Red's arms shot up and he held them back.

"No!" he cried.

"Let 'em alone, Red," growled a deputy, trying to push Red's arm down. "I don't approve o' lynchin's an' you know it. But this is one time I ain't stoppin' anybody as wants to do it!"

Red whirled and pushed the crowd back.

"But I am! No matter what he's done, he deserves a fair trial—especially with the facts of the case the way they are."

"What you talkin' 'bout?"

The crowd relaxed and Red stood back, taking a deep breath. Sheriff Parks, he knew, would never permit a lynching.

"The man sittin' there with his face half shot off is a friend o' yores. Leastwise, he was until he got into a shootin' scrape which was none o' his business."

"That's crazy talk!"

Red passed over the interruption and continued:

"He was mindin' his own business when he heard about the sheep war last year, which—" Red said, looking at the faces about him with a twinkle in his eye, "some o' you might be rememberin'."

The posse didn't laugh, but only looked puzzled and, Red noted with relief, were slipping guns back into holsters.

"At any rate, this miserable hombre decided you cattle-men was fightin' a just fight and joined up with you."

"We all took our chances," put in Lem Parks.

"True," replied Red. "But y'all was fightin' for some-

Red Faced the Werewolf

thin' that meant somethin' to you. This hombre was only fightin' 'cause he thought you was in the right. You see, he ain't no cattleman!"

There was a surprised silence for a moment. The ranchers looked at each other with raised eyebrows. Red felt something tug at his chap and looked down to see Little Beaver standing beside him.

"What you leadin' up to, Red?" asked Sam Locke.

"Wal, this hombre joined up with you and fought side by side with you," Red went on. "He did a lotta damage to those sheepmen until one o' them caught up with him. They threw some lead at each other, got in close evidently, and the sheepman's gun went off in his face."

He pointed down at the bandana, flapping lazily in the breeze of the late afternoon. The werewolf man clutched it to his throat as all eyes focused down on him for an instant.

"That 'bout the way it was?" Red asked.

The man nodded.

"You can see for yourself," said Red. "He keeps his head covered to hide the half o' his face blown away!"

A startled gasp broke from the men's throats, and Red could see their eyes soften in sympathy.

"That's enough to drive any man crazy," muttered Zeth Todd.

"Shore is!" breathed Harky Walters, and bit off a man-sized chaw of tobacco from a brown-black plug.

"That's exactly what happened," continued Red. "He

went plumb stark loco and fetched up this werewolf disguise. He's been killin' ever since, not knowin' what he's doin' half the time."

"Well, who is the critter?" asked Sheriff Parks.

"Clay Lerner!"

At the mention of the name, the man on the ground began to thrash about, kicking and beating the ground with his feet and hands. He rolled over on all fours, raising his head to the sky and howling.

The men watched him, speechless, shuddering at the wolf cry that had terrorized them and brought near disaster to the valley. Their fingers strayed warily to their guns.

Red grabbed a lariat from one of the frightened cowmen and bound the prisoner securely, hands and feet. The cattlemen relaxed and let their hands drop.

"Get yore hands up—all of you!"

They whirled in the direction of the voice—a woman's voice!

"Keep away from those guns. Yo're covered and I shoot straight!"

It was Rita Lerner, standing on the ledge from which her husband had jumped into Red's trap. In her steady hands were Red's six-shooters. She held them resting on her hips, fanned apart to take in the entire group. She nodded shortly toward her husband, who was looking up at her silently with a wild fanatical light in his eyes.

"Untie his feet!" she commanded.

Red lowered his hands and bent to do her bidding. He fumbled at the ropes for a moment, then suddenly jerked Clay Lerner's legs, pulling him forward and around in a lightning move.

A jet of flame darted from the gun in the woman's hand. Red felt hot lead crease his cheek. But the next second, he was behind her mad husband, using him as a shield.

"All right, Mrs. Lerner, drop those guns! Yore next shot at me is gonna nick his hide 'stead o' mine!" shouted Red from behind the broad back.

The woman's guns lowered a trifle, but immediately sprang up again as the posse men moved to their own irons.

"Get back away from Clay and Red—all o' you!" she cried.

They obeyed slowly, giving ground only when her guns moved threateningly. All moved back except Little Beaver who stood resolutely a few feet from Red.

When the men were backed to the slope, the scene froze as though chiseled out of stone. The posse stood with hands hanging limply at their sides, knowing that even the slightest movement might mean a bullet through the heart. Clay Lerner seemed to have regained a measure of sanity and he sat quietly looking up at his wife. Red crouched behind him keeping a firm grip on his shoulders.

The only motion was the slight wave of Rita Lerner's

torn dress in the breeze.

There was death in the air, and it hung at the tips of her trigger fingers.

The possemen pitied the poor woman and her unfortunate husband, yet they could not let her help Clay to escape. They decided on caution, for they knew her guns would smoke if they made a move.

CHAPTER VIII

ESCAPE

It became a waiting game. As the sun lowered in the west and tricky shadows played over the rocks, the odds slowly switched away from Rita Lerner. Soon the twilight mantle would blend the men before her into the ashen rock. She would be the only visible figure, standing out above them, framed in the starlight.

Then she would be the target!

She saw this as well as they. If she was to act, she had to do so surely and quickly. Her tortured brain sought vainly for the way. If only she could drop down from the ledge on to the shelf. She thought of jumping, but knew that in the few seconds it would take her to reach the ground and regain her balance, the posse would have the drop on her.

It wasn't likely they would shoot a woman, but men battling for their lives can move mighty fast. One of them would be on her almost the moment she touched ground, tearing the guns from her hand.

Poor Clay! Look at him sitting there—his eyes begging to be set free. Of course it was wrong! All wrong! Clay was mad. He had killed for the lust of killing, getting some horrible pleasure in imagining himself a werewolf. Rightly, she should let them take him—kill him! It was

123

the only fate a demented creature such as he deserved.

But her happy years of married life before the tragedy filled her mind. Those years served as an unbreakable bond between them, and if death was to come, she decided they would go together.

The shadows deepened and she had to strain forward to see clearly the faces and hands of the posse. It was almost too late . . .

"What are you going to do, Red?" Her voice rang with emotion.

Red's soft chuckle came to her through the dark. " 'Pears to me like that's up to you, Rita—'less you wanta be reasonable."

"I'll do anything, Red. Make any bargain with you. But I won't let you take Clay!" She spoke with desperate finality.

Red didn't answer. He knew it was just a matter of time.

Sheriff Parks' deep bass broke the stillness after a moment. "Put up yore guns, Mrs. Lerner, an' I guarantee Clay here will get a fair trial."

"I can't, Sheriff. There ain't a jury on earth that wouldn't convict Clay—an' rightly," she said quietly, but bitterly. "But I'm his wife an' I'm standin' by to see no jury ever gets a chance at him."

There wasn't a man there who didn't admire the loyalty and spunk of the woman, but not one could side with her. The fiend who was her husband had too much

blood on his hands—the blood of their friends and families.

The shadows lengthened—a moving curtain of black
swept toward them as the sun finally dropped below the
horizon. Suddenly the massed figures of the men were
no more; the small sturdy figure of Little Beaver seemed
to melt before her eyes and the spot where her husband
was sitting with Red shielded behind him, became a black
blended blob.

The guns wavered unsteadily in her hands. Panic gripped her. A thin whistling sound stirred the stillness and
her body grew tense. A lariat hoop dropped over her
body and jerked hard causing her to cry out. The sudden
jerking motion pinned her arms to her side; the guns
dropped from her hands. She fell sobbing to the ground,
pulling at the rope, trying to break from its firm em-
brace.

There was movement below; the sound of hard boot
heels on the solid rock; strained voices; the incoherent
mutterings and screeches of Clay Lerner who, when the
tension had snapped, began to roll and kick.

Rita Lerner ceased struggling, weak and exhausted
from the long fruitless vigil. She lay quietly, her fingers
loosely clutching the rope when Lem Parks finally
scrambled over the ledge and kneeled at her side.

There was no exultation in the party when they led the
bound prisoners back toward civilization. All, of course,
felt great relief that never again would the deadly wolf

cry echo in Wolf Creek Canyon, but the sobbing grief of
the lone woman going back with her husband to witness
his certain death, silenced their tongues and made their
hearts heavy.

Red Ryder and Little Beaver rode beside the Sheriff
and Lem Parks. They talked quietly of many things.
Red and Little Beaver told of their experiences during
the previous day and the long horrible night. They all
wondered about the skeletons in the basement of the
Lerner house and decided to ride back the following day
and try to identify the unfortunate remains.

"What happened in the Canyon last night?" asked Red.

Sheriff Parks sighed and shook his head. "Two more
killin's. Tom Blake an' Andy Rivers got it this time."

"Blake and Rivers? Their ranches is over east 'bout
twenty miles ain't they, near sheep country?"

"Yeah, what of it?"

"Doesn't it 'pear peculiar to you how Clay could have
covered so much ground durin' a single night on foot?"
muttered Red. "How was they killed?" he asked, without waiting for an answer to his first question.

"Knifed—just like Jeb Weston," replied Sheriff Parks.

"Any tracks?"

"Lots o' 'em, an' all wolf."

Red's lips puckered and he rode along silently for
awhile.

"I'm certain Clay didn't do it, Sheriff."

"I been thinkin' the same thing," grumbled the old

law man. "But all the evidence points against him. The wolf tracks an' that blasted howlin' was just like him."

"Everything but one thing," observed Red. "Clay Lerner's killin's was mad attacks where he clawed and bit just like a wolf. In his mind he was a wolf and he didn't need any weapon. Jeb Weston, Blake and Rivers were killed by knives."

"It do look peculiar," admitted the Sheriff. He spat his wad of chewing tobacco out and glanced sidelong at Red's sharp features. "I don't suppose you'd be havin' any ideas as to who it might be? That is," he added hastily, "pervidin' it don't happen to be Clay."

A grim smile lifted the corners of Red's lips.

"Mebbe I have, Sheriff," he retorted, "an' mebbe I haven't.

Both men chuckled inwardly, each knowing full well they both suspected the same man. If it was he, they knew they would have a tough time proving anything. Jeff Wilkins was a shrewd cutthroat who covered every underhanded move he made so well, that no one had ever been able to prove anything against him.

For years, bloody trails had led right up to Jeff's doorstep and then stopped. Always the final piece of evidence disappeared—an eye-witness would be killed on the eve of a trial, or incriminating papers would mysteriously vanish from the Sheriff's safe. And Jeff Wilkins would go free, walking among the townspeople he was out to fleece for every cent they had, the maligned figure of a man asking from them sympathy for the terrible "insult" to which he had been subjected.

It was an old story to Red and Sheriff Parks. They knew of course, that the actual dirty work was carried out by a gang of cutthroats he kept around him.

Could it be that Jeff Wilkins was using these cutthroats to take advantage of the werewolf scare? Was it a foul plan to rid Wolf Creek Canyon of cattlemen?

When the posse reached Zeth Todd's house, it was decided that they would spend the night there and finish the trip early in the morning. A crackling campfire was soon going outside, and Mrs. Todd and Zeth barbecued a spit of juicy steaks. The tantalizing aroma had the hungry posse swallowing their tongues to keep them from hanging out, as they waited for the meat to get done.

The sudden contact with civilization, with human beings; the familiar atmosphere of a peaceful, well run home; the sound of many voices, affected Clay Lerner strangely. Securely bound to a tree so that he couldn't escape while the posse relaxed its vigil, he stared at the comfortable scene with longing eyes. There was no trace of the "werewolf" nature now; he seemed in every respect sane and docile.

Zeth Todd had furnished him with some old clothes, and to outward appearances he looked like a bear of a man with the nature of a kitten. The only discordant note was the bandana wrapped around his face to cover the ugly cavity on one side.

Sitting at his feet, hugging his bound legs was his wife, quietly crying. His odd voice murmured words of comfort, begging her to forget about him, to understand that never again could they have a happy life together. But in this mood of sane understanding he was again the husband she knew—the man she loved; all the misery, the horrible nightmare of the past months was forgotten.

"I can't let them take you, Clay," she cried. "There must be some way out!"

"I don't want no way out, Rita. I'm sane now—know what I'm sayin' an' thinkin'. But one o' those spells might come up on me any minute, startin' with pains in my head, gettin' worse every second. Finally gettin' so bad I can't stand it no more an' then I don't know what happens!" He looked down at his wife miserably. "But you know an' they know—I KILL!"

"But you don't mean to. You don't know what you're doin'!"

"That ain't no excuse. Fact is, I kill!"

"But maybe a doctor—" Rita offered hopefully.

"Too late for that now. Like Red Ryder said when he caught me, there's too much blood on my hands." Squirming in the tight bonds cutting into his wrists and legs, he sighed heavily. "I gotta take my medicine, Rita, an' no matter what, you gotta let 'em give it to me."

"I can't!"

"You got to! Even if I go mad again, you mustn't do one single thing to help me. If I try to escape, warn 'em!

Make 'em shoot me dead!"

"No, Clay—NO!" sobbed his wife.

"Yes!" he muttered between clenched teeth. "I wanta die. It's the only way I can escape the terrible things I done. If you care anything about me—do as I ask!"

Red Ryder, lying down in the shadows not far away, catching up on some much needed sleep, was awakened by the strained voices and eavesdropped on the conversation. His heart went out to the unhappy pair, but he knew that Clay was right. He would be better off dead. Still, the man was insane—perhaps there was a way out. Over in Houston, Texas, there was an asylum for the insane. Maybe Clay could be sent there. He would talk to Sheriff Parks about it in the morning.

Other thoughts crowded Red's mind as he tried to doze. Somehow, his conversation with Sheriff Parks kept repeating itself. Those knife killings . . . Jeff Wilkins . . . sheep grazing in cattle country . . . Jeff Wilkins again . . . his cold-blooded cutthroats. One thought chased after another faster and faster until finally, exhausted, he fell into a fitful sleep, tossing and muttering incoherently.

Sometime later, he awoke clammy with sweat. In his mind was a plan. How it got there, he didn't know. Maybe he dreamed it, or in that half world between sleep and wakefulness, he had logically figured it out. At any rate, as he sat up, wide awake, going over each detail, he knew instinctively that it was right and worth the chances involved to carry it out.

Quickly he got to his feet and moved between the sleeping figures around the smoldering embers of the campfire, searching for the Sheriff's large, rotund body. He spied it alongside his son Lem, knelt by his side and touched the shoulder gently. The next instant, he felt cold iron pressed against his forehead.

Red chuckled.

"Put up yore gun, Sheriff. It's only me, Red Ryder."

"Red? Oh!" Sheriff Parks snorted and wheezed angrily. "What in thunder's the idea o' wakin' a man up outuva sound sleep like that?"

"Sorry, Sheriff," answered Red, an amused smile on his face in the dim light of the dying embers.

"I mighta plugged you right through yore blasted red head," admonished the grizzly law man. "Yo're lucky I didn't shoot first an' ask questions after!"

He returned his gun to its holster beside his head and yawned prodigiously.

"Wal—whadaya want?"

"I got a plan," replied Red quietly.

"A plan! For Pete's sake, can't it wait till mornin'?"

"We better talk it over now, 'fore the others start stirrin'. It needs a lotta workin' out."

Grumpily, Sheriff Parks groaned to his feet and walked away from the circle of sleepers toward the tree where Clay Lerner was tied. Red followed. When the posse had turned in for the night, Rita Lerner had been taken into

the house and locked in a room with windows barred
so that she could not help her husband to escape. Clay
had been bound at the foot of the tree so he could sit
down and rest against it.

When they silently approached, he was sleeping sound-
ly. They examined his bonds and found them secure.

Leading the way to the rear of the house, the grum-
bling Sheriff turned to face Red.

"Now what's this gol-blasted so important plan o' yours
which can't wait till mornin'?"

Red began to talk eagerly. The Sheriff's sleepy eyes
blinked and were wide awake. A devilish look came into
them and he began to chuckle deep in his throat.

Red went on, unfolding each carefully planned step;
now and then the Sheriff would interrupt to ask a question or make a suggestion. They spoke for a long time
until in each of their minds was a clear-cut plan of action.

When dawn broke, the camp stirred. Mrs. Todd
opened the door of the house and the exhilarating odor
of bacon and eggs wafted from inside to tantalize fresh
appetites. One by one, the sleepers sat up, yawned,
stretched, scratched their tousled heads and looked
around.

Among those stirring was Sheriff Parks. His eye twin-
kled brightly with the thought of what was to come.

"Hey! LOOK!" Sam Locke was pointing to the tree
to which Clay Lerner had been bound. *"He's gone!"*

The startled posse gaped at the empty tree, their mouths

sagged open in disbelief. There was a mad scramble to examine the dangle of ropes at the foot. Harky Walters got there first, picked them up and slid them through his fingers, as the others pressed around him. He held up two cleanly severed ends.

"They've been cut!"

CHAPTER IX

DECEPTION

An angry growl broke from the lips of the men. For a moment they glanced suspiciously at each other. Sheriff Parks grabbed the cut ropes from Harky's hands and studied them intently. A string of expletives issued from his lips and he turned to face his posse.

"Whatever rat done this is gonna pay plenty," he said dangerously.

Without another word, he pushed roughly through the men and stamped toward the house. They followed, grim looks upon their faces.

Zeth Todd came to the door yawning.

"Mornin', gents!" he smiled.

"Where's Clay's woman?" demanded Sheriff Parks without returning the salutation.

Zeth gazed back at him in astonishment.

"Ain't she in her room where we locked her up?" he asked in puzzlement.

"How in tarnation do I know?" thundered the Sheriff, shoving him aside and storming into the room.

The officer of the law hurried through the kitchen and living room of the comfortable rambling house toward a closed door. Trying the door, he found it locked. Zeth and the other cowmen crowded after him.

"Give me the key."

Mrs. Todd squeezed through holding out a large iron
key. "Here 'tis, Sheriff."

He grabbed it from her hand, jammed it into the lock
and turned. With his foot, he kicked the door open. "If
yo're in there, come out, Mrs. Lerner!"

There was no answer.

Muttering more harsh words under his breath, the angry law man strode into the room. His sharp old eyes
peered into every corner and fell on an open window.
Through it, he could see the stable. A soft breeze lazily
rustled the pongee curtains. The boards that had been
firmly nailed across the window were gone.

"She's beat it—right out from under our noses!" roared the irate Sheriff.

He whirled about to face the unbelieving men who
crowded the doorway. The utter impossibility of the escape had them mentally floored and they stared back at
him with dazed eyes.

"Mebbe if we hurry we can catch 'em," someone suggested after a moment.

The Sheriff silenced him with a cold, scornful frown.
Suddenly his brow puckered and he stepped forward,
scanning the faces before him.

"Where's Red Ryder?" he demanded.

No one knew.

A quick search proved Red wasn't around the house.
Confirmation of the fact that he had disappeared along

with Clay and Rita Lerner came when it was reported that Little Beaver was missing too.

"Where in blazes did that red-headed beanpole wander off to with that half-pint heathen o' his?" blustered the Sheriff, pacing up and down inside the kitchen. "He should have more sense than to run out without sayin' a word! 'Specially now when we need 'em to go after that lunatic an' his wife."

Sam Locke, who had been leaning against the fireplace stroking his beard in deep thought, suddenly pushed himself away and sauntered into the center of the room. The Sheriff stopped and looked at him.

"Well?"

"It shore looks bad for Red in my opinion," observed the bewhiskered cowman.

"*Bad?* What you drivin' at?" demanded the Sheriff.

"Red seemed mighty anxious to save that lunatic's neck when we all wanted to string him up yesterday," he answered.

"Go on," said the Sheriff. "I'm listenin'."

"I was just thinkin' that mebbe—an' I *mean* mebbe— Red an' Little Beaver might o' had somethin' to do with the escape."

He stopped for a moment to see how his words were taking effect. Stony faces stared back at him, but there wasn't one objecting voice. "Might be a good idea to turn the posse on Red for a change an' see if we don't turn up the Lerners too."

There wasn't a man in that room who didn't owe something to Red Ryder. His generous helping hand had pulled them out of tight scrapes; several of them owed their lives to him. In each one was imbedded loyalty and respect for the man who was not there to defend himself.

Sam Locke saw the hostility gleaming in the faces about him and covered up quickly.

"Course it's just a thought an' probably there ain't nothin' to it. I just been thinkin' around an' tryin' to figure out—," he said lamely.

"One o' these days yo're gonna think once too often, Sam Locke," muttered Harky Walters, who not only owed his life to Red Ryder, but his ranch and the cattle on it as well.

"It goes without sayin' Red Ryder had nothin' to do with the escape," stated Lem Parks defiantly.

Sheriff Parks lowered his head and thumbed his leather vest pockets. There was a shrewd look in his shaded eyes as he moved slowly across the room. Brushing past Zeth Todd, he looked up for a second. The two men exchanged quick looks, but their faces were masks. A silent message seemed to pass between them.

Turning, he said, "Mebbe we're lettin' our hearts rule our minds 'bout Red. Mebbe Sam's right!"

The assembled ranchers gazed at him in astonishment. Red's closest friend, Sheriff Parks, making a statement like that! It was hard to believe. For that matter, it was hard for the Sheriff to utter it. Meeting the antagonistic

eyes was the hardest task of all. But it had to be done—
and with authority.

"I know what yo're all thinkin', but I'm workin' for the
law an' when I got no other clues, I gotta follow what I
got!"

"But, Dad—" protested his son, Lem.

"No 'buts' about it, son. Even if it was you an' things
looked suspicious, I'd hound yore trail till I caught you."
He hitched up his belt and passed through the dumb-
founded posse toward the door. "Come on," he shouted.
"We're ridin' after Red Ryder!"

Sam Locke was the first to follow him. A pleased look
was on his face and his chest stuck out importantly. The
rest followed uncertainly, gazing with disgust at the
swaggering figure—with wonder at their Sheriff.

Some hours before, when Red Ryder and the Sheriff
finished their powwow at the rear of the house, it was
still over an hour to sunup. The plans they had made were
clear in their minds and they proceeded to carry them
out.

First, by tapping lightly on the Todd's bedroom window, they awoke their host and his wife and quietly
gained access to the house. Quickly, they outlined their
plan, impressing upon the rancher and his wife the need
of absolute secrecy. The Todds eagerly agreed and promised full cooperation.

They awoke Rita Lerner, who was at first frightened
and refused to do anything which might further endan-

ger the life of her husband. However, when Red mentioned the possibility of sending him to an asylum in Houston, new life seemed to well up within her, the dullness dropped from her eyes; they seemed to sparkle in the dim moonlight penetrating the room.

Exercising the greatest care in removing the boards from the window, the deception of her escape was accomplished.

The hardest part was yet to be accomplished. Clay Lerner had to be awakened. A question ran through all of their minds: *would he be sane?* In the event that his madness came upon him before they were away from the ranch all their efforts would go for naught.

Rita volunteered to wake him.

"He won't be surprised at seeing me. At least it will be less of a shock to him," she explained.

From a window, they watched her steal silently around the circle of sleeping men into the dark shadows of the tree to which her husband was bound. Then all they could see was a vague blur where she knelt. They waited, straining their eyes through the dark. Seconds ticked by. Nothing happened. A warm feeling of success came over Red.

A minute later, Rita appeared in the bright moonlight and hurried across the open stretch to the house. When she was close, they could see a happy smile on her face.

"He all right?" asked Red anxiously, as she rushed into the room.

"Perfectly!" replied Rita; her voice bubbled with joy and excitement. "I told him what you said about the asylum in Houston and—and, he almost cried he was so happy!" Tears for the joy she felt lit up her eyes.

"Does he know that he's got to stay bound up just in case—?" questioned the Sheriff, his voice trailing off.

"Yes. He even insists upon it. He asked me to remind you to bring more rope so you could cut those that now bind him."

Zeth Todd went to the corral and saddled up horses while Red went to awaken Little Beaver. The Indian boy was wide awake in an instant and following Red into the house without question.

They all waited for Zeth to come back before going to the tree to release Clay Lerner. The rancher returned in a few minutes carrying the extra rope.

"Everythin's set," he told them. "Horses saddled up an' waitin' just back o' the stables."

Silently, the small party proceeded outside and hurried to the tree. Clay Lerner greeted them silently. Red's sharp bowie knife cut into the ropes binding him. Stiffly he rose to his feet, rubbing his numbed wrists.

"Ain't got a bit o' feelin' in 'em," he remarked.

"We ain't got time to let you get feelin' back, Clay. Be sunup soon, an' we gotta get 'way from here 'fore then," said Red, holding out the fresh rope.

The prisoner stared at the rope. An electric tension suddenly filled the atmosphere. Sheriff Parks and Zeth

They Slipped Away Before Dawn

dropped their hands to their guns.

"Clay!" Rita hissed in a frightened whisper, as she saw the look on his face.

The wild eyes continued to stare at the rope. Red moved forward, holding it in front of him as though nothing were wrong.

"Let's get it over with, Clay," he said quietly.

"Is what you told Rita 'bout the asylum in Houston the truth, Red?" whispered the man hoarsely. It seemed too big a break for him to get.

"I wouldn't 'a' said so if it weren't, Clay," replied Red evenly.

Clay was silent. His eyes lifted from their morbid contemplation of the rope and looked steadily into Red's.

"If it ain't, I'd rather make a break for it now, Red, an' let you drill me."

"It's the truth!"

Clay was silent a moment.

Slowly, the prisoner lifted his wrists.

"I believe you, Red," he said.

There was a sharp letting out of breaths as Red wound and tied the rope securely.

A few minutes later, the party was on its way, heading back to Needle Rock. The Sheriff, Zeth and Mrs. Todd watched them out of sight with a prayer in their hearts that the maneuver would work.

When the sun came over the horizon and the posse awoke to find Clay Lerner had escaped with his wife—

Sheriff Parks and the Todds were more surprised than anyone.

At least, it appeared that way!

The sheriff smiled to himself as he heard the posse members muttering angrily at Red's apparent desertion.

CHAPTER X

Upon reaching Needle Rock, they made their way up the slope and through the pass to the cave. Dismounting before it, Red helped Clay Lerner from his horse, then pushed the massive boulder aside.

It was getting light, but the cave was just a horrible black hole as they stood on the outside looking in. Red unhooked the lantern from his saddle where Zeth Todd had the foresight to hang it, lit it and led the way inside. The only sound was the cheerful gurgling of the fresh-water spring in the middle of the floor.

"Well, this is it," said Red, facing Clay and Rita. "Little Beaver an' me has got to be movin'. We got a lot of work to do."

"How long will we have to stay here, Red?" asked Rita in a small, frightened voice.

"Not too long," replied Red, not wanting to state any definite time, since he had no idea how fast his plan would work. "Leastwise, you'll be comfortable here when the Todds bring up beddin' and food and things."

"We'll stick it, Red," said Clay. "You just get that Jeff Wilkins dead to rights this time. He's one hombre Wolf Creek can do without *plenty!*"

He didn't have to say more. If there was any living

man who had just cause to hate Jeff Wilkins and pray for his downfall with all his soul, it was Clay Lerner. There he stood, a grotesque, horribly disfigured man, looking forward to spending the balance of his life in an insane asylum. If any man was to blame for this and the mad killings which he had committed, it was Jeff Wilkins, the avaricious force who had sold out his lifelong friends, the cattlemen, engineered the sheep war, and caused death and destruction throughout Wolf Creek Canyon.

"We'll get him this time, Clay," vowed Red. "If I ain't missed my guess, he's overplayed his hand and I aim to prove it!"

The cowboy and his little Indian companion started to leave. When they were in the entrance, Rita Lerner suddenly called them.

"Red, what if the Todds don't come?"

Red turned, smiling.

"They'll come, Rita, don't worry 'bout that," he assured her.

"I guess I'm just nervous—sorry."

"I'm closin' up the entrance when I leave," Red informed them after a moment. "I think it best."

"Must you?" cried Rita in a scared voice.

"He better. I'm gettin' one o' my headaches," muttered Clay, tightly. "Tie up my feet too, so I can't storm around."

Red hurried out to his horse for his lariat. When he re-

turned, Clay Lerner was down on his knees. In the sharp
light of the lantern, his eyes shone mad and glazed; his
teeth were bared like the fangs of a wolf; from his throat
came the blood curdling cry of the wolf.

Rita started toward him.

"Keep out o' his way!" shouted Red. "I'll handle him."

The madman concentrated on Red. He snarled and
crawled toward him, using his bound hands as a prop,
giving the impression of a three-legged animal.

Red moved fast, circled around and came up behind
him. In a few seconds the thrashing legs were bound
from the knees down. Clay struggled on the floor trying
to free himself, howling, squirming.

Rita bravely knelt by his side, tried to stroke his fevered
brow. He snapped at her hand, butted her with his
head. There was nothing to do but wait—let the fit pass
off. Red Ryder picked Rita up and walked her to the
far side of the cave.

"Let him be, Rita. It'll pass off soon."

"If there was only something—!"

Helplessly, they watched until finally, exhausted by his
vain efforts to free himself, Clay fell into a tortured sleep.

"He'll be quiet now, Rita. Just keep out o' his way
when he gets like that an' keep him bound up," advised
Red. "We gotta be goin' now."

"Hurry back, Red—please!"

Pushing the boulder back into place, Red Ryder and
Little Beaver mounted their cayuses and rode again for

Zeth Todd's ranch.

Though Little Beaver hadn't said one word since Red
had awakened him, his sharp ears had gathered frag-
ments of conversation which gave him the general idea
behind Red's plan. At first he had been frightened riding
with the man who, but a few short hours before, had been
their deadly enemy—the cause of their hurried trip back
to Wolf Creek Canyon. However, his calm quiet during
the ride to Needle Rock, reassured him. The fit in the
cave gave Little Beaver another start, and it was upon this
that his mind dwelt as they sped back to the Todd ranch.

"Red Ryder!"

"What is it, young 'un?" called Red over his shoulder.

"What if werewolf man get loose and find way out
from cave like us?"

"We're takin' that chance," was Red's short reply.

Though this was a remote possibility, it bothered him,
but there was nothing to be done about it.

As they neared the ranch, they saw a large cloud of
dust several miles ahead. It was Sheriff Parks and the
posse heading back to Wolf Creek, as planned. Red would
follow in an hour or so. Meantime, he decided, Little
Beaver and he could do with a stack of wheat cakes and
honey, by courtesy of Mrs. Todd.

As they reined up in front of the ranch house, Zeth
Todd was leading his sturdy-legged mustang and a pack
horse around the side. The pack horse was loaded down,
almost staggering under its load.

" 'Pears to me you got everything on that critter 'ceptin' the barbecue pit, Zeth," laughed Red, jumping to the ground.

"Shhhh! Don't say it so loud. Mrs. Todd might make me take that too!" chuckled Zeth. "How y'all feeling?"

"Fit! Everythin' go off all right?"

"Perfect! You shoulda seen Sheriff Parks," grinned Zeth, shaking his head. "I swear, he shoulda been an actor on the stage."

With keen amusement, the rancher told Red and Little Beaver about the morning's events. Red and Little Beaver roared at the picture of the blustering Sheriff and the befuddled posse.

"But there's one hombre I'd advise you to keep a weather eye on, Red," said Zeth suddenly serious. "He turned mighty sharp on you."

"Who's that?"

"Sam Locke. He's one cattleman who ain't been too unfriendly to Jeff Wilkins either."

Red pondered this. Sam Locke had been acting sort of strange. He recalled their conversation over Jeb Weston's grave. Sam had been mighty scornful of Red's opinion that there was no werewolf and that there was a deeper reason behind the killings.

Naturally, up to this point, Sam had not been entirely wrong. Clay Lerner, in a manner of speaking, had become a werewolf. But that didn't explain the knife killings of Jeb Weston and the others. Red was certain in his mind that the werewolf disguise, the tracks and the howling were mere subterfuge—staged to blame the killings on Clay Lerner.

"Wal, I gotta be on my way," grunted Zeth Todd, pulling himself into his saddle. "Guess Clay an' Rita is gettin' mighty hungry an' can use some o' this grub I'm packin'."

Mrs. Todd came out to see him off and admonish him to be careful.

"An' now," she said, turning to Red and Little Beaver when Zeth was gone, "you two wash up an' I'll have a mess o' wheatcakes ready when you come in."

"Mrs. Todd—you practically read my mind," chuckled Red.

When Red Ryder and Little Beaver rode into Wolf Creek several hours later, hot and dusty from the journey, they noticed puzzled looks on the faces of the townspeople, as they went up the main street. Their friends greeted them guardedly as though not wanting to be seen talking with them. At the far end of the street, a group of men poured out of the Sheriff's office, and lined up—blocking the road. Their hands rested on their guns.

Leisurely, Red and Little Beaver walked their horses toward them. People rushed by and darted into buildings, taking up positions by windows to watch what had the makings of a rip-roaring fight.

Though Red's face was a grim mask, inside he was enjoying himself. The Sheriff had certainly done a perfect job in turning public sentiment against him. This of course was exactly what Red wanted. Upon this resentment was based the success of his plan.

Reaching a point ten feet in front of the Sheriff and his posse, Red and Little Beaver stopped.

"Howdy, Sheriff."

"Don't you 'howdy' me—*traitor!*"

Red's jaw squared and his eyes narrowed to steely slits.

"That's a mighty irritatin' word, Sheriff."

"If it fits you, wear it!"

"Ordinarily, I'd plug any man who called me that 'fore he had a chance to explain. Seein' as we been friends for years—I'm givin' you a chance."

"I don't need to explain nothin'," retorted Sheriff Parks. "Any hombre who'd endanger the lives of every man, woman an' child in this section don't deserve explanations."

The two men's eyes locked. Maybe it was some dust, maybe not—but their eyes winked ever so slightly at the same time.

"If yo're speakin' o' Clay Lerner an' his wife—I had my reasons for lettin' 'em go," offered Red bluntly.

"I'm not interested in no reasons. You helped a prisoner escape an' I'm holdin' you responsible," roared the Sheriff.

A keen onlooker to this dramatic meeting was Jeff Wilkins, who watched from the porch of his bank.

"Yo're not holdin' me, Sheriff," replied Red quietly.

"There ain't a man amongst you got the nerve or ability."

"Big words, Red Ryder, but I'm one hombre who ain't skeered o' you," retorted Sheriff Parks, starting to move toward him.

Red sat quietly in his saddle watching the burly figure approach. Little Beaver, whose pony stood a few feet behind Thunder, let his eyes steal sideways toward banker Wilkins.

The look on the banker's face was reassuring.

"Red Ryder an' Sheriff better makeum good fight," whispered the Indian boy between tight lips. "Wilkins look like he thinkum you bluff."

Red heard the muttered warning and so did the Sheriff, who was now alongside Red's saddle. Suddenly his hand darted up, grabbed Red's holster belt. Red came tumbling from the saddle to sprawl on the ground. Thunder whinnied and backed away, looking startled at the two men he knew were fast friends.

The Sheriff followed his advantage, diving at the prostrate cowboy and landing on him with a thud that almost took Red's breath away. Red jammed his hand into the lawman's face, forcing the head back and loosening the hold around his neck.

Feeling his advantage gone, Sheriff Parks swung his fist hard against Red's arm, knocked it away and lunged for Red's neck again. Red, however, had moved with the speed of lightning, rolled out from under the two hundred and fifty pounds of muscle and bone, and jumped

The Posse Feared Red Ryder

to his feet.

Moving with tremendous speed for a man of his bulk, the Sheriff scrambled to a standing position just as Red dròve in at him. Stinging blows flicked into his face. Though the blows looked real enough, Red managed to glance them off the cheeks so that their full weight was not felt, but hard enough to cut and bruise.

The grizzled lawman didn't give an inch of ground even as blood dripped from his lacerated face. Jamming bearlike fists into Red's chest, he managed to get in close, ducking his head low, out of sight.

"Clip me on the chin! Knock me out!" he panted hoarsely. "Then make yore break!"

Red fitted action to the words. Feeling more pain for the deed than the Sheriff probably felt from the blow, he let loose with a jolting uppercut to his friend's chin. The lawman's head snapped, his knees buckled; he rose up on his toes, arm bent out, wrists dangling weakly, and crashed forward on his face.

Red's guns were out, fanning the posse threateningly as he backed quickly against his horse to cover himself from behind.

"Now if there's anyone else as thinks he can take me— step forward!" he barked.

The men, though they had their hands on their guns, weren't ready to exchange lead with Red Ryder. Though he was the greatest gun master in the southwest, he had never been known to kill a man. But in this new savage

frame of mind there was no telling what he would do.
From the way he acted, he would have no compunction
about smearing his perfect record with blood.

"Just as I thought—not a man in the lot o' you," he
sneered.

This was too much for Lem Parks. In his blood was
a fighting do-or-die spirit. He wasn't his father's son for
nothing. Not even Red Ryder could question his bravery.

His gun jumped from his holster, but before it had
a chance to clear leather, there was a sharp report—it
dropped to the ground, its barrel smashed. Except for the
sudden jolt from the speed of Red Ryder's bullet, Lem
was unhurt and looking down in mild surprise at the remains of his six-shooter.

"Next time my arm might not be so good case anyone
else gets notions," warned Red. "Now clear the way—me
an' Little Beaver's comin' through!"

As he spoke, Red grasped the saddle horn, put a foot
in the stirrup, but kept his eyes and guns darting warily
over all within range. An accomplished trick rider, when
necessity called, Red hung from the horn, supported by
the single stirrup, swinging low on Thunder's side as the
horse plunged forward.

The posse hastily melted to the boarded sidewalk,
clearing a wide path for Red Ryder and Little Beaver
to gallop through. When they were enveloped in a cloud
of dust streaking for open country, the posse sprang into
action. Pushing into the road, their guns barked a hail

of lead at the fleeing targets.

The shots went wild, though some of them came dangerously close, whistling past Red's and Little Beaver's ears. Crouching low along their horses' necks, they prayed no lucky bullet would get them.

They headed across the mesa toward Wolf Creek, forcing their mounts to the utmost, knowing that in a few minutes the posse would be heading after them.

Back in town, people poured out of the stores and houses into the street. Lem Parks bent over his dad, bringing him to. The old lawman finally sat up, feeling his jaw tenderly and touching the painful bruises on his cheeks.

"He shore packs plenty o' sting in those fists," he muttered almost proudly, then struggled to his feet and tottered to his horse.

"Horses!" he yelled. "We're goin' after him an' we're catchin' the critter this time!"

"Dad, you better stay here," urged Lem, trotting at his side. "I'll lead the—"

"Stay here?" roared the lawman incredulously, pulling himself into his saddle. "Not on yore life, son. I'm gettin' even with that red-headed termite."

The posse thundered out of town. Grim looks were on the faces of the riders. None could figure it out—their friend, their champion, turning outlaw! The last thing they had ever expected was to be riding posse on Red Ryder.

It was a heart-breaking job for all of them, but law and order had to be restored to Wolf Creek Canyon. If Red had chosen to join forces with the other side, he was now their enemy.

No one noticed in the excitement that one of the posse men was missing. When the shooting began, Sam Locke had darted into the back room of the bank to keep a secret appointment with Jeff Wilkins.

CHAPTER XI

WOLF RIDERS

Red Ryder and Little Beaver hit the open mesa, circled around and headed back toward town, keeping behind a row of scraggly cottonwoods. As they neared the outskirts, they heard the pound of hooves and knew the posse was getting started.

Quickly, they reined in, shielded themselves behind a thick clump of trees and waited until the riders passed.

They rode on at a moderate but steady pace, saving their mounts for the long journey.

Red had a definite destination in mind—the hated sheep country. It was his hunch that somewhere, cleverly hidden by the rocky formations jutting into the rich grazing land of this up-country territory, he would find the camp of Jeff Wilkins's cutthroats—their base of operation from which they preyed upon the cattle ranchers, trying to drive them out.

How he was to find this camp, approach it and become a member of the gang was not clear in his mind. Somehow, however, he felt that within a day or so, Jeff Wilkins would get word to his henchmen that Red was outlawed. If and when that happened, Red was confident he would be made welcome in the outlaw camp. Wilkins would feel it quite a feather in his cap to have Red Ryder working for him.

Red had to chuckle at the thought. Naturally, Wilkins might not have been taken in by the dramatic scene put on for his benefit alone before the entire town. He was a clever man and even though the fight and escape had seemed real in every respect, he still might have seen through it.

There was only one thing to do—hide out in the enemy country and watch and wait for developments. During the nights, he and Little Beaver could scout and try to find the killers' camp on their own.

During the day, they passed several ranches but skirted them wide to avoid discovery. Fortunately, they didn't meet anybody on the open range, though they passed many herds of grazing cattle.

Finally, toward sundown, they crossed a rocky divide and entered sheep country. Below them, peacefully grazing, was a large herd of woolly sheep. A sheep dog scurried around as he chased in strays, snapping and barking at their heels to make them hurry.

Red and Little Beaver watched the amusing scene for a while, then, keeping below the ridge, made for a gorge jutting off from Wolf Creek. Their tired horses walked slowly, heads drooping wearily. Rather than push them too hard and risk their going lame, Red decided to camp at the foot of the gorge where a Wolf Creek tributary stream came out of the ground.

They made camp and had a cold supper of jerk meat

and sour-dough biscuits. Though it was getting colder as night fell, they didn't risk a fire, preferring not to reveal their presence until they had had a chance to scout the country.

Weary from the trip, they rested after their cold supper, enjoying the cool, clear beauty of the night. The distant sound of hoof beats suddenly reached their ears.

"Sound like three horses," observed Little Beaver.

"Can't make out which direction they're ridin' from. Can you?"

Little Beaver pointed toward Wolf Creek.

"They'll pass right by here," said Red quietly. "We gotta hide."

Quickly they covered up the evidence of their camp, caught their horses' reins and led them across the creek behind a boulder. Fortunately, the ground at this point was sand, muffling the sound of Thunder's and the Indian pony's hooves.

A few minutes later, three shadows hove into view, galloping down the gorge bed. At first, in the darkness, it was hard to distinguish the riders. There was one thing, however, they could tell immediately—they wore no hats. The reason for this was apparent when they reined in near where Red and Little Beaver were hiding.

Instead of hats, leering wolf heads covered their heads; instead of clothes, they wore dirty grey wolf pelts; and instead of boots, wolf paws were bound to their feet. Each one of the wolf riders carried a long, wicked-looking knife, sheathed in a belt about his waist; the shining steel glinted dully in the moonlight.

"This is where we break up," one of them said, "an' help that werewolf do a little killin'!"

"Yeah," another put in, "an' when we meet back here, three more ranchers is gonna be singin' psalms with the angels!"

Their cruel laughs at this sally echoed through the canyon. Red's blood boiled and his fingers closed on his guns. Little Beaver saw this movement and reached out a restraining hand.

"Not guns, Red Ryder," he whispered. "Use-um lariat."

Red shot the little Indian a grateful look. Swiftly, he detached his rope from his saddle. Two of the men were close together, but the third's horse had strayed off a few feet, making it impossible for Red to get the three of them.

Little Beaver saw this and got busy with his own lariat.

Almost at the same instant, the two ropes whistled through the air, Red's wide loop dropped quietly over the two close together, and jerked them kicking from their saddles before they knew what had happened.

Little Beaver's loop also found its mark, but some instinct had warned the rider so that, as it dropped down on him, his hands flew up to ward it off. Little Beaver yanked with all his might, but the rider yanked harder, pulling Little Beaver out from behind the rock, spilling him on his face.

At the same instant, the rider jammed his spurs into
his horse. The startled animal darted forward. Little
Beaver clutched the rope tenaciously as he was pulled
through the sand. His head and face groveled in it, causing him to choke and splutter. With an effort, he gathered his strength and pulled on the rope with all his
might, at the same time throwing his legs forward to act
as a brake.

The startled horse reared high with the sudden jerk,
unbalancing its rider. Little Beaver gave a final pull and
the man crashed to the ground in a heap.

Red Ryder, meanwhile, had come out from behind the
rock, pulling hard on his rope to keep the loop tight
around the prisoners. They struggled with it, trying to
relieve its biting pressure from their arms, but could do
nothing. Cursing their unknown captor, they pressed
against each other, struggled to their feet and rushed
him.

Red darted aside, flipped the rope and took another
loop around them. He let it drop down their bodies and
pulled tight when it reached their knees. Their legs shot
from under them. Like a pair of Siamese-twin birds, they
flew through the air to crash on their faces in the cold
sand.

Bellowing with pain and rage, wolf heads twisted
awry, they had no choice but to submit to a complete
binding of their arms and legs. Finally, they lay still, tied

up so securely that even their enraged minds had to admit defeat.

Finishing his task, Red hurried to assist Little Beaver, who was dodging and dancing around the third man, holding the rope tight, but having a hard time keeping out of the way of his rushing attacks. With Red's help, the man was soon lying beside his "team mates," puffing and spitting sand.

"That does it, young 'un!"

"Red Ryder an' Little Beaver shouldum stick their own knives in black hearts," breathed the little Indian with savage vehemence.

Red Ryder slowly shook his head.

"No, Little Beaver, our job ain't to kill black-hearted devils like these—just to hand 'em over to the law."

He sat down on a rock, Little Beaver at his feet, looking up at him.

"You see, young, 'un," Red went on, "no man's got the right to kill other men. Killin's mighty serious business, but livin' is even more serious. It's the most important thing a man has. It takes a mighty lot o' heavy weighin' an' considerin' by a whole bunch 'o fair-minded people to decide if a man ain't deservin' o' his life."

"But we know men here gonna kill ranchers," argued Little Beaver. "We hearum say it."

"Still it ain't our job," said Red with finality, "an' we're turnin' 'em over to the law just as soon as we get our little job done."

He Started into the Gorge

"What we do with 'em now?"

"Gag 'em and then toss 'em into a cave till we're ready to fetch 'em," said Red, getting to his feet and going over to Thunder. "Meantime, let's be thankful we was able to stop their killin' more innocent people tonight!"

Red rummaged in his saddle bag and pulled out the torn shirt he had worn during their trip through Needle Rock.

"Good thing I saved this," he muttered. "We can use it for gag cloth."

Tearing the shirt into strips, they efficiently went about the task of gagging their prisoners. This done, Red scouted the gorge wall, and about half a mile down he found a small cave, shielded by a thick growth of creepers from the view of anyone passing below.

Red loosened the ropes around their legs, shoved a gun into their backs and prodded them up the steep incline into the cave. There again he bound them, soaking the knots so that it would be impossible—owing to shrinkage as the rope dried—to undo them.

It was fortunate in more ways than one, Red realized, that they had encountered the killers. Since they were just starting on their assignment of death, their headquarters could not be far off.

Leaving their own mounts and the captives' horses to graze in a secluded knoll, they made their way afoot along the gorge, keeping to the shadowed walls, stopping every now and then to listen.

When they had traveled about half a mile, the gorge took a sudden turn and beyond it the narrow ribbon of water flowing along its bed widened. The gorge walls became higher. The moon, riding the sky low in the east, hardly touched the depths of the gorge, and so they advanced in darkness.

Despite this disadvantage, they managed to make good time, the ground being fairly level, though rocky and treacherous in spots.

Soon, in the distance, they could hear the tumbling waters of Wolf Creek, which in reality was no creek at all, but a fast river filled with rapids, falls and innumerable sharp bends.

"The camp can't be far off now, Little Beaver," whispered Red.

"We better takeum easy or mebbe we run into sentry," warned the cautious little Indian.

Red nodded and moved his holsters to the front. They went on, proceeding with the utmost caution, their trained ears listening for any warning sounds.

Suddenly, Red looked up. A man stood at the top of the gorge, rifle cradled in his arms, peering down into its dark depths. Red grabbed Little Beaver, shoved him against the wall and pressed himself as flat against it as possible.

The man continued to peer down—seemingly right at them. That he didn't see them was a miracle. Obviously, he had heard them. After several minutes, he straightened up, moved on and disappeared from their view.

"Whewwwww!" breathed Little Beaver.

"Lucky for us it's so dark down here. Otherwise he'd 'a' spotted us shore as shootin'," remarked Red. "Let's go—!"

The nearer they came to Wolf Creek's roaring waters, the quicker the blood pulsed through their veins. Rocks and shadows became tricky in the dim light, taking on weird, threatening shapes. The strain on their nerves was almost unbearable, and if they hadn't been made of stern stuff, they would have turned and fled. As it was, the impulse to do so gripped Little Beaver continuously, but he fought it down and crept forward.

Somewhere very near was the camp they sought. Red knew that if he could learn its exact location, he would have a trump card to play at the proper time. The proper time would be when he was ready to break up Jeff Wilkins's murderous gang in a single, daring move.

Up to this point, Red's plan had been vague. Now he was able to plan ahead and take the initiative. Once the location of the camp was discovered, Jeff Wilkins would play the game his way! Jeff didn't know it, but he was going to become Red Ryder's partner!

"Yes, sir!" thought Red, as Little Beaver and he finally detected the red glow of a campfire just ahead; "Yes, sir, now Jeff Wilkins and me is shore enough gonna become partners!"

They rushed forward and dropped to the ground, flat

on their stomachs at the edge of a steep precipice. Far below them, a huge fire licked at the sky, its leaping flames lighting up the entire ravine. A row of roughly assembled log cabins lined the far precipice. Adjacent to them was a corral in which half a dozen horses were crowded together.

Around the campfire squatted the men Red and Little Beaver were looking for. They knew each one of them well—men who had been caught up in Jeff Wilkins's web and were now his slaves, stealing, killing and doing all of his dirty work. They were a knavish crew and seemed to revel in their illegal assignments.

It had long been Red's ambition to wipe them out and now he felt that soon this would be realized.

"Can you remember this place, Little Beaver?" whispered Red excitedly.

"Shore!"

"You better. Yo're comin' back here mighty quick," said Red with a soft chuckle.

Little Beaver looked at Red queerly, but didn't ask questions. He had learned that when Red talked crazily, it was best to leave him alone and wait for the answers.

"Come on, let's get goin'," said Red, after they had watched the quiet camp for a while. "We've got work to do."

"*Not so fast, Red!*"

Red and Little Beaver whirled around.

"An' get yore hands back from those guns!" the voice

ordered.

Sam Locke's stocky figure slid into view. His beard quivered, and the six-shooters in his hands shook dangerously. Even with the guns in his hands and with the drop on Red, Sam was afraid of him.

CHAPTER XII

"So the posse caught up with me!" said Red, quietly fixing his trembling captor with a cool, unruffled look and slowly raising his arms over his head.

"It's caught up with you—but not the posse yo're thinkin' it is," retorted Locke, edging in to take Red's guns.

Red knew what he meant; he suddenly remembered Zeth Todd's warning about Sam Locke. This, he decided, bore out Zeth's suspicions—proved Locke was a traitor to the cattlemen and in league with Wilkins. However, Red decided to play dumb.

"You tryin' to tell me they got *two* posses lookin' for me?" he asked with mock astonishment.

"Might call it that," retorted Locke, jumping to the rear and jerking Red's guns from their holsters as if they were red hot irons.

Locke's own guns became steady in his hands with Red disarmed; fear dropped from his face and he swaggered to the front to face Red with a triumphant sneer.

Red had to force back a smile that twitched about his lips. How easy it would have been—even disarmed as he was—to turn the tables and smash Locke's treacherous face to a pulp! But that could come later—first of all, he had to find out what Locke was up to.

"Now, Mr. Red Ryder," snarled the man sarcastically, "you an' yore little Indian can do an' about-face and march down into that camp—an' no tricks!"

"Down into that camp?" exclaimed Red, feigning surprise. "Don't tell me yo're intendin' to capture those tough hombres down there too!"

Locke blushed behind his thick beard at the compliment, and bristled importantly.

"Stop askin' so many questions an' poke on down there," he muttered. "Gowan!"

"Yo're shore a brave man, Sam," said Red, slowly turning to obey his instructions. "Smart too. How you ever tracked Little Beaver an' me up here is amazin'!"

Actually—and Red knew it—Sam Locke didn't have the remotest idea he was going to stumble on Red and Little Beaver until he almost fell over them in the dark, hearing their whispered voices. Red hoped he hadn't heard their conversation! That would call for a bit of tall explaining.

Locke took this second compliment even more to heart than the first.

"I ain't nobody's fool," he admitted proudly.

"You shore ain't," agreed Red quickly. "You shore nipped my outlawin' career in the bud."

"What you talkin' 'bout?" Locke asked suspiciously.

Red turned back to look at him in surprise.

"Weren't you in town today when Sheriff Parks an'

me had it out?"

"I was there—what about it?"

"What do you mean—what about it? I'm a hunted man!" Red insisted.

Locke sneered and shrugged his shoulders.

"Don't mean nothin'. You got somepin up yore sleeve."

"I shore have!" answered Red heartily. "Fifteen thousand dollars o' cached money!"

"What?"

"You heard me. Why d'ya think I let Clay Lerner and his wife go? They showed me where it was hid in exchange for his freedom!"

A greedy look came into Locke's eye. He forgot about the guns in his hands and let them drop downward. Red saw this, sprang forward, grabbed Locke's wrists and squeezed with bone-crushing pressure. The startled man groaned, cursed and twisted on his toes, to sink squirming on his knees and let the guns drop to the ground.

Little Beaver instantly scooped the weapons up.

For a moment there was an ominous silence. Sam Locke gazed up at Red's grinning face with hatred and fear; Little Beaver leveled the business ends of the heavy guns at a triangular furrow between Locke's eyes.

Crrunch! A footstep sounded in the gravel behind them!

Red heard and his eyes flashed with a sudden joy. Someone was hiding in the dark, listening. Red's mind raced; he began to talk fast.

Sam Locke Was Caught by Red

"You made a fool move lettin' yore guns drop, Sam. I was just gettin' ready to cut you in for a half share, if you'd let me go."

"Yo're lyin'!" croaked Sam.

"If you wanta behave, I'll still cut you in for a *quarter* share," replied Red, ignoring Sam's retort.

"Why?"

"I need help."

"Now I knew yo're lyin'. You never asked help from no one!"

For the first time in his life, Red Ryder regretted his enviable reputation for self-sufficiency. Throughout his career, until Little Beaver had entered his life, he had always traveled alone, asking help from no one, but giving it to all who were in need.

Now, ironically, in the face of this gigantic bluff, his reputation was working against him. But he was determined somehow to convince Sam Locke that he spoke the truth—that he needed help, but more important, he must *convince* the unseen eavesdropper.

All this flashed through Red's mind as he stooped and took his own six-shooters from Sam Locke's belt where the traitor had stuck them.

"Suit yoreself, Sam. Little Beaver an' me'll do just like we was plannin'—mosey back along the trail and camp until Jeff Wilkins comes along."

An odd glimmer came into Sam's eye.

"Yo're thinkin' o' tyin' up with Wilkins' an' his gang?"

he questioned.

"With Wilkins, yes. But I want no part o' that gang o' his," returned Red, matter-of-factly. "This'll be a *private* deal 'tween Jeff and me."

"How come you picked out Wilkins?" asked Sam slyly. "I thought you hated him."

"Personally, I do. But when it comes to business I can afford to overlook a few things."

Red was purposely letting Sam question him freely. He wanted the eavesdropper to hear his answers and have a chance to think them over.

"Another thing," muttered Sam. "How come you to find this camp an' how come you think Wilkins comes here?"

"I've known 'bout it for a long time. Matter o' fact, I followed Wilkins here over a year ago," lied Red; and chuckled, "only he didn't know it!"

Sam Locke seemed puzzled, even disappointed. With every word, Red was smashing his own reputation— painting himself a lawless renegade who used his good deeds as a cloak to cover his real operations.

"I can't figure you out, Red," sighed the man on the ground.

"Seein' as yo're not gonna be around much longer," said Red in a voice suddenly edged with steel, "it don't make no difference how you figure me!"

"Whadaya mean?"

"You asked too many questions, Sam. Then you made

the mistake o' lettin' me answer 'em. *Now you know too much!"*

This was Red Ryder's grand gesture, made to convince the man in the shadows. He drew his gun from its holster, dragged Sam to his feet and held him in an iron grip.

"Say yore prayers, Sam," he hissed into his face. "And say 'em quick!"

"No, Red! . . . Don't! . . . I promise I'll never talk. Honest!"

"Say yore prayers," repeated Red.

"Red!—*Please!*"

Again Red heard a foot crunch in the gravel. Now was the time! He shoved Sam from him with all his might, and coldly watched the figure stagger back, flaying the air with his arms and gazing with blood-shot eyes at Red's rising gun.

"Hold yore fire, Red Ryder!" ordered a familiar voice through the dark.

"Who's there?"

Dropping to one knee, Red whipped his other gun out, leveling it in the direction from which the voice came.

Little Beaver, who had watched Red's strange performance with growing amazement, finally understood. He too recognized Jeff Wilkins's voice; knew that Red had been talking to *him* instead of to the quaking, worthless Sam Locke.

Wilkins stepped out of the dark, slipping his guns into his holsters. A wide grin racked his pudgy, sagging face.

"I guess you an' me has got some business to talk over, Red."

Red's mouth dropped open and he slowly let his guns drop down.

"Wilkins!" he exclaimed, putting as much surprise into his voice as he possibly could. "So you been back there in the dark listenin' to everythin' I had to say to this yellow-livered hombre!"

"Didn't miss a word, Red," grinned the crooked banker. "Especially that part about hating me!"

" 'Tain't somethin' you didn't know," retorted Red.

"No—guess not. But you come mighty close to gettin' a bullet twixt yore eyes," said Wilkins. "Mighty close!"

"Now I'd shore like to know what stopped you." Red got to his feet and holstered his guns. "It couldn't 'a' been somethin' I said to Sam, here—could it?" He looked hard at the crafty face of Wilkins.

"Reckon it was, Red. Somethin' 'bout Clay Lerner's fifteen thousand dollars which you and me was to split."

"You got mighty sharp ears when it comes to money talk, Jeff," replied Red. "Too sharp! I don't recollect speakin' 'bout any *split*."

"You know I wouldn't be interested in anythin' less than a fifty percent share, Red." Wilkins's voice carried a threat in it.

"You ain't worth it, Jeff," stated Red flatly.

The muscles in the banker's face grew taut, the flabby jowls quivered. This was exactly what Red wanted. By arguing over the non-existent money and the shares they were to get, he was automatically erasing any doubts which Jeff Wilkins might still have in his mind. Red figured that upon thinking it over, the banker would finally agree to taking one-third of the money, but plan to shoot Red in the back once he found out where it was cached.

The men argued and haggled over the terms of dividing the "loot" for some time, like a pair of Oriental traders. Red enjoyed this play-acting.

As Red foresaw, Wilkins finally did accept a one-third cut. And when he struck the bargain, a deadly smile lurked about his lips.

"Get down to camp, Sam—an' not a word o' this to anyone!" ordered Wilkins.

Sam shuffled off.

Red again feigned surprise.

"You mean Sam here is one o' yore gang?"

"Yep!" laughed Wilkins. "Shave off that beard o' his an' he's got one o' the meanest-lookin' faces on the face, o' this earth. I use Sam to keep me informed on what the cattlemen are cookin' up behind my back. Haw! Haw! Haw! Ain't that a slick stunt?"

Red joined in the laughter, but his heart was filled with loathing for the traitor. It was going to give him particular pleasure to see Sam Locke behind bars. Sam, who was supposed to be a loyal cowman, playing spy and snooper for the enemy chief! Red wondered how long Locke had been on Wilkins's payroll.

CHAPTER XIII

LITTLE BEAVER ON HIS OWN

The bearded scoundrel turned and made his way down the narrow, winding trail into the ravine below. The single trail was just wide enough, Red noted, for a single horse to pass, making attack on the camp almost impossible. It could be made only from the heights of the ridge and this would not be very effective since there were plenty of protective rock formations scattered at the bottom to provide cover from every direction.

There was only one obvious method of attack that could be at all likely to succeed, and that was a long-drawn-out siege. Red frowned at the thought of this and wondered why Wilkins would pick out a place where he and his men could be trapped so easily. It wasn't like Wilkins to take chances, mused Red—not like him at all.

"I think I'll go down an' visit my boys for a moment," said Wilkins, interrupting Red's train of thought. "They had a little job to do tonight an' I want to make sure it come off like I planned."

Red and Little Beaver knew of course to what "little job" he referred and smiled inwardly at the remembrance of the "wolf" killers, now bound and gagged in a cave up the gorge.

"Okay, Wilkins, but hurry up. We got a long trip 'fore mornin'," replied Red putting into his voice irritation which he didn't feel.

Actually, the cowboy was grateful for the opportunity to give Little Beaver instructions and work out the final details of his plan to dispose of Jeff Wilkins and his entire gang once and for all!

When the banker was out of sight heading down the trail, and his footsteps could no longer be heard on the hard rock, Red Ryder took Little Beaver aside.

"I've gotta talk fast, young 'un, so listen close."

Little Beaver nodded.

"Yo're stayin' here," Red continued. "I'll trump up some reason or other to tell Wilkins. I want you to scout around an' find out if there's another way out o' that ravine down there."

"Must be," put in the little fellow. "Ravine big trap this way."

"That's the way I figure it. Now when you find the other entrance, ride back to Wolf Creek and head the posse here fast as possible. I'll be waitin'."

"Why you no capture Wilkins now?" asked Little Beaver.

" 'Cause I want to find out a few things from him first," answered Red. "There's a lotta killin' 'round here that needs explainin' an' I got to get Wilkins to start braggin' 'bout how he done 'em—*leastwise,* how he planned 'em so his gang could do 'em."

"Me catchum what you mean!" said Little Beaver with a big grin. "Once you learnum secrets of werewolf knife killin's, Wilkins gonna swing by neck!"

Red returned the grin and clipped Little Beaver playfully on the chin.

"Somethin' like that, young 'un. But I gotta find out where all his papers and things is cached so's he don't have no loopholes this time when we bring him to trial."

Their sharp ears picked up the sound of returning footsteps.

"Okay, Little Beaver," Red whispered quickly. "Meet you here with the posse by sun-up."

"You betchum!"

Wilkins hove into sight, puffing and wheezing. Despite his weariness from the hard climb, a gruesome smile was on his face. Reaching the top he led the way to the horses tethered in the black shadows of the gorge.

"You an' Little Beaver can ride Sam's horse double till you pick up yore own cayuses," he said, grunting as he lifted his heavy body into his own saddle.

"Little Beaver's staying here," replied Red.

Wilkins's eyes narrowed.

"What you tryin' to pull, Red?"

"Nothin'," answered Red quietly, "but I'm still makin' shore my back trail's covered."

They eyed each other stonily. Red could see consternation in Wilkins's look. After awhile, the crook let his gaze drop, shifted uneasily in his saddle and unconscious-

ly darted quick glances toward the trail up which he had
just climbed.

"Okay, Red," he muttered angrily. "You win. I'll tell
my boys to stay here."

"You can do it from here," said Red, fingering the
mahogany handles of his guns. "Just yell down to 'em.
They'll hear you."

"But—"

"No *buts,* Wilkins! It's my way or not at all, Savvy?"

The disgruntled gang leader heaved himself down
from his horse and trudged over to the edge of the
chasm. Cupping his hand to his mouth, he yelled instructions to his henchmen, who looked up at him, their
faces small and blurred in the distance.

"And tell those men waitin' on the trail to mosey back
too," ordered Red. "You ain't been lookin' over that way
for nothin'."

"There ain't nobody—" began Wilkins indignantly.

"Just yell down there and tell 'em to pick up their feet
and bring 'em down hard so's we can hear 'em," inter-
posed Red dangerously. "I'm gettin' a little tired o' this!"

Wilkins's teeth ground together, but the sight of Red's
hands hovering over his guns silenced any further pro-
test. His face looking even blacker than the dark night
warranted, he growled to the men on the trail:

"You heard him, boys—get on back to the camp!"

The clop-clop of high-heeled boots, striking against
hard rock and fading into the distance brought a huge

smile to Red's face. He winked at Little Beaver and
swung himself into the saddle of Sam's Locke's horse.

"Keep an eye down there, young 'un," he said with another wink. "An' hightail it after me case any o' those
hombres think Wilkins was kiddin'!"

The small Indian boy nodded and silently indicated
that he understood and would carry out *all* of Red Ryder's instructions. Red felt uneasy leaving him open to the
dangers which seemed hidden behind every rock. He
felt reassured, however, remembering the keen knowledge of woodcraft which was Little Beaver's heritage
from his Indian forebears.

Instinctively, Little Beaver sensed danger; his sharp
ears and sensitive nose could quickly detect it. No white
man—not even Red Ryder himself—could outsmart Little Beaver when it came to tracking. And last of all, Red
reassured himself, if danger did somehow get within
striking range, Little Beaver was a mighty fine shot with
his small but powerful bow.

Red followed Wilkins into the dark recesses of the
gorge, leaving Little Beaver crouching on the ledge gazing after him.

As soon as Red and Wilkins disappeared and the soft
crunch of their horses' hooves faded into the night, Little
Beaver got busy. His soft moccasin soles making no noise
on the rock, he sped down the narrow trail, keeping his
eyes peeled in front for the slightest movement and stopping every once in awhile to listen for the sound of re-

turning footsteps. He reached a point near the bottom where the trail widened, and from where he could clearly see the faces of the men about the fire.

Their voices drifted up to him, sounding hollow and fuzzy as they bounced off the high walls. For a moment the strange distortion of the voices frightened him, lest they be spirit voices, but he quickly realized they were echoes and proceeded cautiously, keeping close to the wall and in the shadows away from the flickering reflections of the campfire.

Almost at the bottom of the trail, he stopped and listened intently. Two men were arguing. One of them, a big rawboned fellow with a slicing scar across the width of his face, was insisting that they follow Wilkins and Red Ryder anyway. The other was Sam Locke, who was arguing that it was too risky.

"I'm tellin' you yo're wrong, Blogerman!" he stormed at the big man. "Wilkins told us to stay here an' I'm stayin'. If we cross up Red Ryder, he'll not only kill Wilkins—he'll get every one o' us too!"

"Ahhhhh, you yust be skeered!" growled the man called Blogerman, with a Swedish accent. "Aye crack him with my own hands in two!"

The other men around the fire roared with laughter at this brave assertion. Little Beaver hidden in the shadows had to smile also. He well knew that Red Ryder could take on any three of the rowdies and make short work of them, the big Blogerman included.

Little Beaver Was Left on Guard

Blogerman finally plumped himself down on the ground disgustedly.

"You bane yust a bunch o' lilies!" he shouted in his odd sing-song accent.

"I'd rather be a livin' lily than fertilizer for 'em," someone answered and the laughter redoubled, booming against the high walls.

While the men below were busy kidding Blogerman, Little Beaver slipped down the trail, reached bottom and sped, crouching low, behind a row of rocks toward the cabins. He had a hunch that in the back of one of those cabins, built against the high rock wall, he would find the avenue of escape Red Ryder had instructed him to locate.

The entrances to the cabins, he noted, were in plain view of the men around the fire. In order to get into them, he would have to chance being seen. It was a dangerous risk, but time was short and he had to take it.

Dropping flat on his belly, he inched his way into the open, slowly squirmed forward and kept fearful eyes on the boisterous, unsuspecting cutthroats. The man Blogerman was sitting with his back to Little Beaver and more or less blocked the vision of the men on the far side of the fire. Little Beaver counted on his own smallness and dark skin to blend with the brown earth and make him almost invisible in the flickering light.

Moving only inches at a time, he finally gained the door of the first cabin, coiled himself into a ball and dove

through, somersaulting into the room. For a few seconds
he hardly breathed, looking carefully about him, piercing the darkness and noting every detail of the room.

When the trip-hammer beating of his own heart
quieted, he heard the labored breathing of another person. Crawling on hands and knees he approached the
bunk where the man lay. On the way his hand touched
something long and hard—grasped it. He felt the familiar
weight of a branding iron and breathed more easily.

The man sleeping in the bunk groaned and turned
over. His grimy hand dropped over the side of the bunk,
almost brushing against Little Beaver who was right
alongside. The Indian boy ducked just in time and
watched the huge human paw swing like a pendulum
and then hang lifeless—stubby fingers stretched out in a
clawing position.

With cool, calculating judgment, Little Beaver rose
to his feet, lifted the branding iron high over his head,
and swung with all his might. He knew that this was
brutal, but it had to be done.

The relaxed body of the sleeping man seemed to relax
just a bit more; his breathing became quieter—less even.
Fortunately, nobody else was in the cabin.

Little Beaver hurried to the back of the room and felt
along the wall. He searched its entire length but could
find nothing. Certainly, there was no cave leading out of
that room!

Back at the door again, he dropped to his stomach and

began crawling toward the next cabin, slightly larger than the two flanking ones. There too, fortunately, it was dark and if there were anyone inside, he was probably sleeping. Little Beaver continued to clutch the branding iron which had served him so well, and dived into the doorway, peeping out to see if he had attracted attention. Obviously he had not—the outlaws were still around the fire kidding the big Swede.

Turning back into the room, Little Beaver noticed a dim light coming from what seemed to be the distance. Blinking his eyes, he peered more closely and saw the cave entrance he was looking for. The light came from inside the cave and with it he caught the sound of several voices and the whinny of a frightened horse.

For a moment the Indian boy stood in his tracks, uncertain of his next move. He could retreat and try to make it up the trail from which he came; or he could hide under one of the bunks until the men in the cave came out, then sneak in, take one of the horses and escape through the secret exit.

It was upon this latter course that he finally decided. He had to save time and this was much faster—even though the risk of being caught was much greater.

At the approaching sound of high-heeled boots on the cave floor, Little Beaver scurried under one of the roughly built bunks and waited. From his position on the floor, all he could see were men's boots when they finally walked into the room.

The man in front carried the lantern, walked to the middle of the room, and placed it on the table.

"Guess I'll turn in," he said and Little Beaver gulped with fear, clutching his branding iron more firmly. "I wonder what happened to Pete an' Sawyer. They shoulda been back by this time!"

"Mebbe the ranchers they tried to kill tonight didn't scare so easy an' turned the tables on 'em," the other outlaw replied with a gruff chuckle.

"I'd shore hate to have their dirty job," muttered the first man, with a grunt, dropping into the bunk under which Little Beaver was hiding. "Rigged up in that werewolf disguise, they musta killed five men in as many days."

"Yeah," grunted the second, shuffling toward the door. "Me too! Bein' in their shoes ain't no picnic. But you gotta hand it to Wilkins. He takes advantage o' every trick. Who else woulda thought o' dressin' our boys up like werewolves an' lettin' 'em get out an' *help* the real one who's been chawin' people up for the last week?"

"Wilkins is smart, all right," agreed the man on the bunk. "But somethin' tells me he's gonna slip one o' these days an' we're all gonna get it in the neck."

Little Beaver listened to this cold-blooded conversation while he seethed inside. With his own ears he was hearing a confession which proved beyond doubt that Wilkins was the man behind the lawlessness of Wolf Creek. If only Red Ryder could hear!

The man at the door went out; the man on the bunk rose, lowered the lantern, returned to his bunk and was soon snoring peacefully. When Little Beaver was sure the outlaw was asleep, he pulled himself from underneath the bunk and slowly rose to his feet, keeping steady eyes on the still figure and raising the branding iron over his head. With sure aim, he brought it down with the same effective results as before.

Picking up the lantern, he hurried to the cave entrance. Once inside he turned up the wick and rushed forward toward the sound of horses' hooves, stamping on hard stone. Fifteen feet farther on, he came upon a large room. In the center was a long pine board table covered with papers. Though he was unable to read, Little Beaver could tell by their look that they might be important and gathered them together, tying them in a bundle which he slung to his belt.

He noticed as he pushed across the room to another corridor, a small iron safe, fitted into a crevice in the rock wall. He paused, looking up at it for a moment, trying to decide what to do about it. He was certain that in that safe were all the papers Red and Sheriff Parks would need to convict Jeff Wilkins once and for all.

After wracking his brain for some way to take it with him, he realized it was impossible. The safe was much too heavy and would only delay him even if he did manage to get it down from its hole in the wall.

He entered the second corridor, which made a sudden

turn to the right. Quickly he lowered the wick of his lantern, upon seeing a light in the room beyond, in which the horses were corralled. Putting the lantern on the floor, he crept forward, clutching his branding iron and feeling a cold chill creeping up his spine. The Indian lad was brave, but he knew he had little chance, fighting grown men. Yet he couldn't turn back now.

The horses munched straw, flicked their tails and stamped the ground uneasily. Little Beaver felt their uneasiness—sensed that something was wrong. The cayuses knew something, all right.

For several minutes, he stood rooted to the spot, hoping the danger would pass or at least, whatever it was, that it would show itself.

Nothing happened.

Feeling the weapon in his hand inadequate, Little Beaver placed it quietly on the floor, slipped his bow from his back, drew an arrow and nocked it. With the bow and arrow held at his side, ready for instant action, he crept forward. Instinct told him to drop to the ground. He did.

Crrack! . . .

Zi-ing!

A bullet whizzed over his head.

A puff of smoke behind a rock rim—a pair of beady eyes over it. Almost at the crack of the gun, Little Beaver's arrow was speeding to a spot between the beady eyes.

Little Beaver watched its flight with a prayer in his heart. On him depended whether or not the outlaws could escape through their emergency exit. If they could, all of Red's plans might be worthless.

CHAPTER XIV

SHOWDOWN!

Red Ryder, jogging along at Jeff Wilkins's side, just a bit behind in order to keep a sharp eye on the wily crook, was not too sure how things were going to work out. Wilkins was pretty angry because Red had seen through his plan to have a few of the outlaws follow at a safe distance and at a signal, as soon as he had learned the hiding place of the cached money, bear down on the unsuspecting cowboy and kill him.

Now, if there was any killing to be done, Wilkins would have to do it himself. Looking at the overfed, pouchy man, Red had cause to smile. But that wasn't the important thing. Somehow, he had to get back into Wilkins's good graces and make the man talk.

Passing out of the gorge and over the rim dividing sheep country from cattle country, they put spurs to their horses and at a fast canter hit the wide plain—heading cross country toward Needle Rock.

After an hour's riding, they stopped at a water hole to rest their horses. Wilkins lit a cigar and rested against a tree. The expression on his face was still dark.

Red watched him out of the corner of his eye as he crouched by the water hole and scooped up a drink. The crooked banker's scheming eyes gleamed coldly in the dim light of his cigar, darting right and left as though gauging the speed of his thoughts.

During the entire trip, neither man had spoken. The silence weighed heavily on both of them. Red decided to break it.

"Want me to fill yore canteen?" he asked in a friendly voice.

"Huh?" grunted Wilkins, stirring in surprise at the sudden sound of Red's voice. "Oh! My canteen! Shore, an' thanks."

Red went over to Wilkins's horse and reached for the canteen hanging from the saddle. His back was to Wilkins so that his body shielded the saddle from Wilkins's gaze. Alongside the canteen was Wilkins's saddle bag, bulging slightly. Red let his hand wander underneath the flap and feel the contents as his other hand detached the canteen from its hook. The feel of parchment papers met his exploring hand—papers such as wills and contracts are drawn upon.

Ordinarily, finding such papers on a banker's saddle would be commonplace, but, wondered Red, what were they doing there at night when Wilkins was on his way to the camp of his outlaw band? Why weren't the papers in the bank's safe?

The answer to this question didn't require much conjecture. Even as Red turned back to the water hole with the canteen, he knew Wilkins's secret—*THE SECRET OF WOLF CREEK CANYON!*

It was all so clear now, so terribly simple! How Wilkins operated, kept records of his shady deals at the camp
and at the same time kept a legitimate front at his bank
in Wolf Creek.

Red stooped at the water hole and absently dipped the
canteen beneath the water. The cheerful gurgle as the
water rushed in, echoed Red's thoughts. No longer did
he just have to *know* that Wilkins was crooked and be
able to do nothing about it—now he could find all the
evidence to *prove it!*

Red realized, however, that there was a great deal more
to proving Wilkins's guilt than merely producing papers.
If Wilkins was able to do his dirty work in what appeared to be a legal way, there must be someone else with
the legal power to help him, working behind the scenes.

Only one man in the town of Wolf Creek had this
power—Judge Bates! Red didn't know the judge very
well—hadn't had much occasion to talk to him. But
thinking of Judge Bates stirred a memory in the back
of Red's mind. Old Judge Harrison—as fine an old gent
as Red had ever met. Too bad he had had that accident
and . . .

Accident?

Red straightened up; the overflowing canteen trembled
in his hand. He remembered the judge had gone out for
his daily ride one afternoon, but hadn't returned. A
searching party found him the following morning at the
bottom of the canyon, evidently thrown from his horse

and dashed to death on the sharp rocks below.

Suddenly it was all quite clear to Red. At the time of the judge's death, Jeff Wilkins was just getting started as the town banker. A man of Wilkins's distorted ambitions could not get very far with a judge who was honest as the day was long. No!—Wilkins needed his own man in there, someone with the power to sign papers and make things legal with no questions asked!

Bates, Red remembered, had been a none too successful lawyer before his appointment to the judge's seat. He had always seemed to Red rather weak and unforceful. For Wilkins's purposes, however, he was perfect.

The trickery which the two men had practiced on the unsuspecting cattlemen was too complicated to go into at the moment. One thing was plain—Wilkins probably had complete records of everything at his outlaw camp. In his bank, of course, he kept innocent-looking contracts, deeds, wills, and so forth, so that prying eyes could never question his integrity. But the *real* documents—the ones which he used to enslave the cattlemen, keep them bankrupt and indebted to him—were hidden at the camp, legally executed by his empowered accomplice, Judge Bates.

Red's impulse upon thinking all this out was to shout a joyous cry to the heavens and then throttle the low specimen of humanity who for the time being was his "partner." Instead, he returned the canteen to its hook on Wilkins's saddle.

"I guess we better get goin', Wilkins."

"Yep," grunted the banker getting to his feet and brushing himself off. "We got 'bout thirty miles to do tonight yet."

Red grinned.

"Yo're wrong, Wilkins. We ain't got no more than ten miles to do."

"But I thought you said Needle Rock. That's thirty miles from here if it's a foot!" insisted Wilkins.

"I guess I didn't tell you—we ain't headin' for Needle Rock."

"No—where then?"

"Back to yore camp!"

If Jeff Wilkins felt surprise or suspicion he didn't show it. Red kept his eyes on the man's hands which were brushing the dirt from his pants, dangerously close to the tied-down holsters under his black frock coat. Red had heard that Wilkins, despite his bulk, was a fast man on the draw, faster than any man in his gang. This probably was the reason he was still living and leading a gang of such ruthless outlaws.

Still, Red made no move for his own guns.

"You ain't been puttin' one over on me, have you, Red?" asked the banker in a calm voice which told nothing.

"Reckon I have, Wilkins. How does it feel to be fooled for a change?"

"Not much likin' to it, Red," replied the crook, still

brushing himself. "It kinda makes me boil inside."

"Figured it would!"

The next instant, four guns blazed!

Red was down on one knee triggering his six-shooters in a steady roar. Wilkins had dropped to the ground ten feet away and was firing from a prone position. The blinding, savage intensity of a gun fight at such close range could not last long! The targets were too plain—the gunmen too good.

The roaring echoes of the fight rolled across the plain and died in the distance. The great stillness of the night majestically reigned once more. The men were as they had been: Red on one knee, Wilkins prone on the ground. Both men lived and breathed, but there was a sanguine change in their appearance.

A gush of dark liquid spread and soaked the right side of Red's shirt, a gruesome wound cut over his ear. But with it all, he still held his guns trained on Wilkins, a slight haze of smoke curling from the barrels.

The banker was gazing at his hands—or *what had been his hands*. The fury of Red's bullets had concentrated on those triggering helpmeets of death until they were rendered incapable of holding and shooting a gun, of any kind, ever again.

Jeff Wilkins had received the punishment Red Ryder dealt to all who used guns to kill for gain. Never again would those hands feel the warm protective comfort of a six-shooter cradled in their palms; never again would those lightning fingers press a trigger. The hands which had disciplined his gang because of their speed, were useless, unable ever again to perform even the simplest tasks.

Red watched the horrified banker for a moment and then felt blackness closing over him. His tortured, bleed- ing body slumped lifelessly to the ground. The cowboy was feverish and exhausted from the exertion and pun- ishment he had taken the last few hours.

CHAPTER XV

When Little Beaver let the arrow fly at the beady eyes glaring at him over the rock rim, he breathed a prayer and watched. The man behind the rock saw the speeding missile and ducked—but not soon enough!

Glancing off his brow, it stunned his senses and caused him to drop the gun, which he was holding over the rock rim, and topple backwards. Little Beaver uttered a yelp, bounded across the room, scooped up the sliding gun, raced around to the side and leveled it at his would-be assassin.

"Put-um up hands!"

The stunned outlaw looked up in amazement, ruefully felt the bleeding gash on his brow. He winced at the contact and turned burning eyes on his tiny captor.

"Hand over that iron or I'll wallop the livin' daylights outa you!" he growled, starting to lunge at Little Beaver.

Little Beaver didn't budge, but his finger squeezed. Hot lead tore into the man's shoulder. He staggered back, fell hard on his knees, cursed and yelled with surprised pain.

"Why, you—!"

"Makeum one more move an' bullet crease yore head," warned the brave little Indian.

The insane fury died in the man's eyes and he lay groaning on the floor, nursing his dangling arm. Little Beaver saw his other hand grasp for the butt of his second gun. Little Beaver, in a few short bounds, was at the man's side pounding his own gun butt down at the clawing hand. The man roared with the added pain, jerked his hand and rolled over.

Little Beaver grabbed the gun from its holster and hurled it across the room. The other gun he kept, as he ran across the room toward the horses. He picked out a sturdy-legged roan which looked sleek and fast, vaulted to its bare back, turned its head toward the next corridor and urged it forward.

Behind him he heard the shouts of the men and clatter of running feet. The shots and the thunderous roars of pain from the wounded man had attracted the attention of those outside.

Little Beaver felt his stomach do a series of flip-flops; a rock-like lump swelled up in his throat. One by one, using stealth and caution, he was able to cope with these ruthless murderers, but to tackle the whole pack of towering, death-dealing men was a different story. He had to get out—and get out fast!

Digging his soft buckskin moccasin heels into the horse's flanks, he cleared the archway into the next corridor, not knowing what lay ahead. His heart skipped a joyous beat—the entire corridor was blazing with light, a series of pine-knot torches placed every twenty feet or

Red Ryder Got the Breakfast

so made it possible for Little Beaver to gallop his mount through the corridor without let-up.

An idea flashed into his mind after he had passed the first torch. He reined up and turned back. Reaching over his horse's neck, he plucked the torch from its receptacle and snuffed out the flames against the wall. Then, galloping forward to the next torch, he repeated the process and so on down the line.

There were five torches in all. Just as he reached the last one, a shot rang out.

Pinng!

A spray of rock dust kicked into his eyes from where the bullet struck. Desperately, Little Beaver grasped the torch and threw it to the ground as he rode. Bullets whizzed over his head and he could hear the pound of horses' hooves behind.

Suddenly, he heard a howl and the loud scream of a stumbling horse. The trick had worked. Trying to hurry after Little Beaver in the dark, the outlaws had forced their uncertain mounts at a gallop. One of the frightened animals had stumbled, fallen; the others were piling up on top—if the noise and confusion were any indication.

Ahead, Little Beaver could see the bright moon riding over the canyon. A few seconds later, he was in the open, pounding along the canyon trail toward Wolf Creek.

In the meantime, Red Ryder lay unconscious for over an hour. As he lay there, Wilkins crawled over to him

screaming with pain, begging him to wake up and do
something about his mangled hands.

Slowly, consciousness returned to the wounded cowboy.
For many long minutes, though he was conscious, he had
not the strength to move. But strength was flowing back;
he felt the beat of his heart accelerate, and then the blood
course warmly through his body, and, finally, an awareness of the pain from the wounds in his side and in his
head.

When he opened his eyes, he saw Wilkins lying beside him, holding his hands high and moaning with pain.
At the sound of Red stirring, the man turned his head
and cried out:

"Red! For the luva heaven, help me—HELP ME!"

Forgetting the searing pain and torture of his own
wounds, Red pulled himself up and stumbled toward
Sam Locke's horse which he had been riding. He found
a clean shirt and a couple of bandanas neatly tucked at
the bottom of the saddle bag. He ripped them in long
strips, formed one into a wad and dipped it into the water hole. He washed the wounded hands clean of the sand
and dirt that had got into them and bound them up
as best as he could. He then lifted Wilkins to his feet,
dragged him to his horse and heaved him into the saddle.

"Where you taking me, Red?"

"I ain't. You know the way to town and if you don't,
yore cayuse does. When you get there, Doc Hawkins can

fix up those hands right," answered Red, not unkindly.

"But what if somethin' happens to me on the way?" cried the beaten crook, showing himself for the coward he was.

"Nothin' will," answered Red, roping him to the saddle so he wouldn't fall off if he passed out. "I got work to do cleanin' up the rest o' yore cutthroats."

"Please don't do this to me, Red." His voice reached a fever pitch. "I'll pay you! Give you anythin' you want— BUT DON'T LEAVE ME ALONE!"

Red gave the rope a final lash and secured it with two half-hitches. This finished, he looked up at the crying, sniveling excuse for a man, unable to hide the contempt in his eyes. Yet he felt sorry for him and nearly yielded out of pity—but not for mercenary reasons.

"I ain't interested in anythin' you got to offer, Wilkins —so get goin'."

He slapped the horse's flank and watched Wilkins ride away, whimpering and pleading.

"How fast the mighty fall," Red muttered and set about tending his own wounds.

It was just midnight when Red reached the ridge over- looking the outlaw camp. He was surprised to see the big fire still blazing but the entire ravine empty of human life.

His sharp ears detected a faint, muffled sound—so faint he wasn't sure he had actually heard it. Curiosity aroused, he pushed his horse down the single trail and reached the ravine to hear the sounds again—only more plainly this time. They seemed to be coming from one of the cabins—and yet they seemed distant as though coming from inside the towering cliff.

A cold fear gripped his heart as he spurred his horse recklessly toward the cabins. One thought kept repeating itself in his mind:

"Little Beaver's trapped—Little Beaver's trapped!"

In front of the center cabin, he reined in and leaped from his mount. Pulling his six-shooters from their holsters and thumbing the hammers—all thought of personal safety gone—he tore through the cabin door straight across the room to the cave entrance on the back wall.

His hard boots beat a rapid tattoo on the smooth stone floor as he rushed down the first corridor into the large room. Finding it empty, he ran to the corridor behind.

He could hear the shouting and cursing of many men, the loud whinny of frightened horses, the excited stamping of their iron-shod hooves on the rock floor and the reverberating sound of gun fire.

Frantically, he rounded the curves in the corridor to bring himself into sight of the corral room. Suddenly he jerked up short; his nerves almost jumped from his skin. A loud howl and the chilling scream of a falling horse beat into his ears and numbed his senses for an instant.

What followed was a nightmare of confusion. The high piercing screams of frightened horses, the shouts of startled men, the thump and clatter as the horses flayed the air with their legs banging against the rock walls with their hooves.

And then the loud cry over it all:

"He got away! . . . THE LITTLE INDIAN HEATHEN GOT AWAY!"

Red felt a stirring rush of emotion which, when it had passed, left him weak and trembling. Staggering against the wall, he smiled weakly and muttered with deep reverence:

"Thank heaven!"

The next instant, Blogerman stumbled into the dimly lit corral, cursing loudly in his native tongue.

"Reach!" ordered Red, who was framed in the archway at the opposite end of the room.

The infuriated Swede stared for one awful moment, dipped, crouched and fell to the floor, his guns blazing from his hips even as he fell, continuing to spit their death as he stretched his arms forward.

Red flattened himself against the wall, triggering fast, as only his steady hand knew how. Bullets kicked up flying stone all about his head, but none found their mark. Blogerman's guns, however, were soon silenced. They lay splintered and useless in front of him. The trigger fingers of his hands were broken. He gazed at them and then at Red with open-mouthed astonishment.

Red crouched to his knee, fingering fresh cartridges into the barrel, waiting for the others to come. He had not long to wait. Darting from the darkness toward the cover of the wall rocks, half a dozen men poured out. Hails of bullets plucked at Red's clothing like a flock of converging bats.

But Red's two guns spoke with more authority than all the others put together. Each bullet found its mark, accounted for one more adversary. One by one they dropped their weapons, clutched at wounded hands, arms or legs.

The room became cloudy with smoke and acrid from the fumes of exploding gun powder. The mounting screams of the maddened horses in the corridor beyond reached a terrible pitch.

The bark of guns, the screams of the horses, the cries and yells of the wounded men and the thrashing, dinning echoes of it all beat back on Red's ears relentlessly.

Suddenly there were no more bullets tearing at him or crashing into the wall behind him. Overtones of the roaring guns rumbled through the corridors for a few seconds, then disappeared. Screams of the horses melted into startled whinnies and cries of the wounded men stopped all together as Red advanced to the center of the room, eyeing each one, making sure no hand was capable of turning a gun on him again.

At sun-up, true to his promise, Little Beaver returned to the outlaw camp with Sheriff Parks and the posse. During the night, as they had ridden, the Sheriff had ex-

plained the entire plan to the dumbfounded men and
each one felt ashamed and foolish for being so quick to
turn on the man they knew in their hearts could not
knowingly do wrong.

Reaching the heights above the ravine, Little Beaver
called the party to a halt, leaped from his horse and
crawled to the rim to peer over.

Sheriff Parks was saying, "Guess we beat Red Ryder
here."

Little Beaver popped his head over the edge, looked
down and gasped:

"That what you think-um!"

"What you seein' down there?" asked the Sheriff,
heaving out of his saddle, as did the other men.

"Lots!"

Little Beaver was not exaggerating. Neatly bound together and lined up in a row were the ten outlaws. Even
at a distance, they looked as though they had been
through a major battle of the Civil War. Red Ryder was
calmly bending over the fire, cooking up a mess of golden
brown flapjacks.

"Hold up a stack for me!" shouted the Sheriff.

Red looked up, grinned and waved them to hurry
down.

* * *

After a hearty breakfast, Sheriff Parks wiped his mustache with a flaming red bandana, smacked his lips and
turned to Red.

"Well?"

"Well—what?"

"'What!' he asks," cried the Sheriff looking around at the faces of the posse men as though Red's modesty were hopeless. "You know darn well—*what!*"

Red chuckled and put his arm affectionately about Little Beaver. "All right, Sheriff—all right! But yo're gonna get a big surprise."

They all looked at him expectantly.

"You ain't thankin' me for roundin' up these hombres and breakin' Wilkins's gang," he continued, "yo're a-thankin' this little heathen o' mine here!"

"What?"

Little Beaver blushed uncomfortably.

Red quickly told how Little Beaver had found the secret exit, trapped the outlaws in the cave when they chased after him, so that all Red had to do when he came on the scene was blast the guns out of their hands.

When everyone insisted, Little Beaver modestly told his experiences in detail and they listened silently; admiration shone from every eye for this boy with the courage and skill of a grown man.

Red Ryder was proud—very proud. His arm tightened about the Indian boy's shoulder and he was happier, he thought, than he had ever been in his life.

The papers Little Beaver had taken from the table, the deeds and documents in the safe which Red Ryder had found and blasted open, proved over and over again that

Off to New Adventures!

Wilkins and Judge Bates worked in cahoots, lending money to cattle men and making them sign over all their property to Wilkins in the event they should die before the debt was paid off.

"Then that explains those knife killins'," exclaimed the Sheriff when they had gone through most of the papers.

"There ain't no other explanation," replied Red.

"Ah—but we can't prove it!" muttered the lawman disgustedly.

"Don't be so sure o' that, Sheriff."

Sheriff Parks looked up hopefully.

"Don't tell me you—"

"Yep," grinned Red. "Matter of fact, Little Beaver an' me got *three* 'werewolf' killers bound and gagged in a cave up the gorge a piece."

News of the finish of Wilkins and his outlaws spread through Wolf Creek like wild fire. Rejoicing was rampant throughout the town during the day and far into the night.

Immediately, upon returning to town, Sheriff Parks had part of the posse go out to fetch Clay Lerner and his wife, who were still voluntary prisoners in the cave at Needle Rock. At the same time—after seeing that the outlaws and their leader, Wilkins, were safely behind bars—Sheriff Parks dispatched a telegram to Houston inquiring about the asylum for the insane.

When Clay and his wife were brought back to town, an answer to the telegram had arrived. Its message brought real hope to the miserable pair. Clay could count on a peaceful home there for the rest of his life and if his condition could be cured, every effort would be made to effect it.

Red and Little Beaver joined in the merrymaking for a time, then at a mutual sign slipped out into the night.

Thunder and the sturdy Indian pony, which they had picked up on the way back to town, were impatiently waiting outside, tied to the hitching post. At sight of their masters they nodded their heads up and down and whinnied happily.

In a short time, the happy revelry of Wolf Creek faded into the distance as Red Ryder and Little Beaver were galloping over the plains toward new adventure.